D0777560

SPECIAL MESSAGE TO READERS

This book is published under the auspices of

THE ULVERSCROFT FOUNDATION

(registered charity No. 264873 UK)

Established in 1972 to provide funds for research, diagnosis and treatment of eye diseases. Examples of contributions made are: —

A Children's Assessment Unit at Moorfield's Hospital, London.

•

Twin operating theatres at the Western Ophthalmic Hospital, London.

•

A Chair of Ophthalmology at the Royal Australian College of Ophthalmologists.

•

The Ulverscroft Children's Eye Unit at the Great Ormond Street Hospital For Sick Children, London.

You can help further the work of the Foundation by making a donation or leaving a legacy. Every contribution, no matter how small, is received with gratitude. Please write for details to:

THE ULVERSCROFT FOUNDATION,
The Green, Bradgate Road, Anstey,
Leicester LE7 7FU, England.
Telephone: (0116) 236 4325

In Australia write to:
THE ULVERSCROFT FOUNDATION,
c/o The Royal Australian and New Zealand
College of Ophthalmologists,
94-98 Chalmers Street, Surry Hills,
N.S.W. 2010, Australia

MARSHAL LAW

Deputy Marshal Jed Law was sent to Buffalo Crossing to keep the peace; a bloody feud between two ranchers had already cost a man his life. But Law's real troubles started when he first set eyes on Julie Rutherford and her father Ben . . . Opposed by hard cases determined to wipe him out, he would be forced to shoot his way through. And worse was to come . . . Law would need his pistol loaded and ready to use until the last desperate shot.

Books by Corba Sunman
in the Linford Western Library:

RANGE WOLVES
LONE HAND
GUN TALK
TRIGGER LAW
GUNSMOKE JUSTICE
BIG TROUBLE
GUN PERIL

SHOWDOWN AT
SINGING SPRINGS

TWISTED TRAIL
RAVEN'S FEUD
FACES IN THE DUST

CORBA SUNMAN

MARSHAL LAW

Complete and Unabridged

LINFORD
Leicester

First published in Great Britain in 2006 by
Robert Hale Limited
London

First Linford Edition
published 2007
by arrangement with
Robert Hale Limited
London

The moral right of the author has been asserted

Copyright © 2006 by Corba Sunman
All rights reserved

British Library CIP Data

Sunman, Corba
    Marshal Law.—Large print ed.—
    Linford western library
    1. Cattle stealing—Fiction 2. Western stories
    3. Large type books
    I. Title
    823.9'14 [F]

    ISBN 978–1–84617–664–7

Published by
F. A. Thorpe (Publishing)
Anstey, Leicestershire

Set by Words & Graphics Ltd.
Anstey, Leicestershire
Printed and bound in Great Britain by
T. J. International Ltd., Padstow, Cornwall

This book is printed on acid-free paper

1

Jed Law caught the unmistakable smell of trouble the moment he reined up on the outskirts of Buffalo Crossing in south-west Texas. Big-framed and tall, he was no stranger to trouble for he had rubbed shoulders with it for seven years in his job as a State deputy marshal — his plain nickel-silver shield-shaped badge pinned to his shirt under his leather vest. He probed the wide, dusty street with keen brown eyes, right hand resting on the black butt of his holstered Colt .45, and noticed immediately that there were no loungers in the scant shadows along the street, which was unusual in the early afternoon, and he suspected that the bad situation he had been told about back at headquarters was responsible for their absence.

His information had been slight

— no more than that rustling had started a range war between Ben Rutherford, who owned Circle R, and Seth Geest of Big G — and the fact that a man were already dead had brought him post-haste to the edge of Buffalo Crossing, primed for action and ready to go to work. He worked closely with the Texas Rangers on occasion, and they had passed on information that Butch Rainey, the notorious cattle thief, was at work in the area with his Mexican counterpart Pancho Vasquez — who between them handled most of the rustling north and south of the Mexican border.

The afternoon sun was high in the cloudless blue vault of the heavens and heat packed the town with ceaseless torture. Law lifted his left hand and pushed back his dusty Stetson to wipe sweat from his brow. He spotted a saloon on the right, about halfway along the street, and moistened his lips as thirst was kindled by the thought of a cool glass of beer, but the sense of impending trouble prickled in his mind like a burr under a saddle blanket — he could feel the pressure of it, and curbed his need and steeled himself to think of duty before pleasure.

The grating of wheels attracted his attention and his head jerked around as he looked over his broad shoulder at the buggy coming along the trail from the west. A young woman was driving the buggy with a much older man seated beside her. Law dragged himself from his thoughts and admiration momentarily softened the harsh lines of his angular face. The girl was something to look at with her lithe figure snug in a black dress and a small black Stetson perched atop a mass of blonde hair. Her face was beautiful despite the deep frown marring her features. She was in her early twenties, Law judged, and the sight of her pleased him immensely, although she presented a sombre picture in her black garb. Then he noticed a .38 Remington in a holster of the gunbelt buckled around her slim waist and his thoughts returned to duty.

The girl's companion had the look of a prosperous rancher about him. Dressed in good range clothes, his weathered face was set in harsh lines, and Law noted that the man had his right arm bound up in a rough sling that was spattered with dried blood, and there were ugly bruises on his features.

Law tipped his hat as the girl passed by and, for a moment, her narrowed blue eyes met his before flickering to take in details of his appearance, but she gave no sign of acknowledgement and went on into the street, her shoulders stiff. Law got the impression that she was burdened with the troubles of the whole world, and the physical condition of her companion bore out his suspicion.

He touched spurs to the dun and followed along the street. There were two horses standing at a hitching rail on the left, in front of a hotel, and a tall man dressed in a dark blue store suit emerged from the building as the girl neared it. She had been reining in towards the sidewalk until she saw the man, and then hauled on her reins and whipped the horse to move away, but the newcomer stepped down into the dust and lunged to grasp her reins, pulling the buggy to a halt. Law slowed his forward movement and continued at a walk.

'Julie, what are you doing, coming into town like this?' The man's voice rasped unpleasantly, his tone laced with anger. He was in his late twenties, broad shouldered and tough-looking, and had a low slung pistol nestling on his right hip in a tied-down holster on a black leather cartridge belt. His heavy features were scowling and he was displeased to see her, his thick lips twisted in a snarl, his dark eyes filled with a bad-humoured glitter.

'Are you telling me that I can't come into town now?' she demanded in a high-pitched tone. 'You stood by while my brother was killed, but you're ready to throw your weight around me. Well it won't work, Crowley. I'm not scared of you, and you'll have to kill me to stop me doing anything I want.'

'I'm only concerned that you'll find more trouble than you can handle,' Crowley replied. 'You don't have any more sense than Dave did, and I'm thinking that'll bring you the same trouble he found. It won't matter that you're a girl, and you should start using your common sense after what happened to your brother.'

'I don't need any advice from a bully like you. Call yourself a law man! Take your hand off my reins and get out of my sight. Your face is more than I can bear at the moment. Pa needs to see the doctor real bad, and no one is gonna stop us doing what we have to, so stand clear and mind your own business.'

'What's wrong with your father?' Crowley had got around to looking at the man in the buggy, who had not moved or given any indication of having heard what was said.

6

'What do you think? Geest's hard cases showed up at the Circle R this morning — Tog Doughty and Hawk Bassell with three other bullies — they threatened Pa before beating him badly, and they had the nerve to tell us to quit Circle R by tomorrow morning.'

'So what's the problem? Do like you're told and there won't be any trouble.'

'I didn't expect you to have any sympathy for us.' The raw emotion in the girl's voice made Law squirm in his saddle. 'All you ever do is stand by and watch while greedy men break the law on all sides. You're useless as a deputy. You can't do the job you're paid for. I sometimes wonder if you're working with the bad men.'

'Geest figures he's got proof that your outfit have been rustling his stock so he's got a right to get tough with you.' Crowley shrugged his heavy shoulders. 'I can't do a thing unless I see the law being broken. My hands are tied.'

The girl swung her whip and lashed out at Crowley, who shrugged and released the reins. She turned the whip on the horse and the buggy went on. Law followed at a walk, reaching Crowley in time to hear him muttering in an undertone but unable to make out what the deputy said. Crowley looked up at him, and then dropped a hand to his holstered gun. Law spotted a silver deputy sheriff star on Crowley's shirt front, which was half-hidden by the lapel of his jacket.

'Say, you're a stranger!' Crowley sounded surprised and his voice grated with belligerence as a glint appeared in his mean brown eyes.

'I won't let that worry me if you don't,' Law responded.

'It's my business to find out what you're doing, showing up here. You got the look of a gun hand about you. Who sent for you, or are you a drifter looking for a job? There's nothing but hard cases showing up in town, all moving in because they've got a smell of the trouble we're getting.'

'You won't have any more success with me than you had with that girl,' Law responded, and saw anger flash into Crowley's dark eyes. 'Who is she, anyway?'

'Julie Rutherford. Say, what's it to you? You better keep your nose out of local business. It ain't safe to butt in where you ain't wanted.' Crowley scowled, his prominent chin thrust out. 'I'm gonna keep an eye on you, mister, so don't step outa line. If you ain't got business around here then keep riding and get outa town.'

'I've got business here,' Law responded. He took a searching look at Crowley's fleshy face, noted a star-shaped scar on the left cheek just under the eye, and something clicked in his mind. He paused while he searched for an answer but nothing came and he touched spurs to his dun, loping along the centre of the street to get closer to the buggy.

Julie Rutherford was pulling in close to the sidewalk in front of the bank and, as she stepped down from the buggy, a man emerged from a nearby alley and approached her quickly. She did not see him, her first awareness of his presence being when he grasped her left arm and spun her around to face him.

Law dismounted from his high saddle and wrapped his reins around the hitching rail in front of the bank. He slapped dust from his clothes, eased the gun belt around his waist, and slipped the retaining strap off the hammer of his Colt .45. At two inches over six feet in height he was a big man and his brown eyes glinted as he listened to the harsh voice of the man addressing the girl.

'What's wrong with your father, Julie?'

'Ask Doughty or Bassell. They beat him up this morning. We've been told to up stakes and pull out for other parts.'

'That's the way they treat rustlers around here. But it wouldn't have happened if you'd let me take you under my wing. I would have kept the wolves off your necks. You're too stubborn for your own good, you know. But I guess that runs in the family, huh? What are you doing here today? I thought you were burying Dave.'

'How long do you think it takes to put a man in the ground?' she demanded bitterly. 'Stay away from me, Leroy Cooper. What I just told Crowley applies to you, only more so. You're nothing but a low-down gunnie, running around with that thug Chance Geest, and you don't fool me even though you pulled the wool over Dave's eyes and involved him in that cattle-raising scheme.'

'I saw you speaking to Crowley. What was he saying to you? You know you don't have to take any notice of him.'

'He gave me the usual guff, and then some, warning me off, but I'm through listening to him. Anyone wants to get their hands on Circle R will have to kill me like they did Dave. I'm through backing down, and I'm gonna make my stand here and now, come hell or high water.'

'That's stupid talk, and you know it. Do you think the killers will care that you're a girl? And why you think I had anything to do with Dave's death beats me. What put that idea into your head in the first place? I'm on your side, if you did but know it. And I don't like the way you keep bleating about me being responsible for the trouble that's come to this range. If you say it often enough then folk will begin to believe there's some truth in it. Why don't you ease off and let me take care of you, Julie? You know I wouldn't let anything bad happen to you.'

'I'd rather take on a snake as a partner before considering you, Leroy! You and Chance Geest! You haven't done a day's work in your lives. All you can think about is raising hell.' The girl's voice shook with anger and she struggled to get free of Cooper's grip but he held her easily, grinning at her ineffectual resistance. 'Didn't you hear what I said? Geest's riders showed up this morning, and warned us off.'

'So Big G's outfit hammer you and you blame everyone else for your trouble! That don't make sense, Julie. If you just say the word I'll take on Geest's outfit.'

'Is this man bothering you, miss?' Law rapped.

The girl turned to look at him, frowning, and the man froze and glanced over his shoulder at Law, his expression changing quickly to anger.

'Who in hell are you?' he snarled. 'What for are you butting in?'

'The lady doesn't appear to want your attention,' Law responded. 'Take your hand off her or I'll do it for you.'

'You better get outa here before you trip over your long nose.' Cooper's handsome face turned ugly and his dark eyes glittered as he dropped a hand to his holstered pistol. 'What's your business in town?'

'Do like I say and I'll answer your question,' Law said quietly.

'The hell you will! Have you hired him, Julie?'

'I'll hire him on the spot if he can use that gun he's wearing,' she replied hotly. 'How about it, mister? Are you looking for a gun job?'

'I can hold my own in any situation,' Law said grimly. 'What's your outfit, miss?'

'Circle R. We haven't hired any gunnies yet, but my brother's murder has changed things. It's time we started arming and defending what we have.'

'I'd admire to work for you,' Law said.

'Then you're hired, and your first chore is to put this two-bit thug in his place. Teach him to keep his hands off me.'

'You heard the boss.' Law did not change his stance but his manner hardened imperceptibly and a tense expression settled on his face. 'Get the hell out of here, Cooper. The next time you reckon to bother the boss you'll have to go through me.'

'Why you — !' Cooper spluttered in fury and backed off a step, his right hand twitching convulsively as he released the girl. The next instant he made a play for his holstered gun, and he was fast. He grasped his gun butt and the weapon slid smoothly upward, rasping out of greased leather. But he halted the movement an instant before clearing his holster, for Law was holding his .45 in his hand, cocked and ready for action, the black hole of his muzzle gaping at Cooper's chest.

'Jeez!' Cooper opened the fingers of his right hand and his pistol fell to the ground.

'You got some sense at any rate,' Law observed. 'But if you reckon my draw was a fluke we can start again. Or you can get to hell out of here. All you got to do is turn around and beat it. I'll leave your gun lying and you can come back when we've gone.'

Leroy shook his head, discomfited by the speed of Law's draw. He took a deep breath and then exhaled noisily before turning on his heel and returning to the alley from which he had emerged.

Law uncocked his pistol and slid it back into its holster. Julie was gazing at him in shock.

'What have I done?' she muttered, shaking her head. 'This is madness! Would you have shot Leroy if he had cleared leather?'

'Sure thing. He would have shot me. But I'm aware that you acted on the spur of the moment, miss, so your offer of a job is not accepted.'

'You haven't done yourself any favours by outdrawing Leroy, and you can bet he'll be waiting for you somewhere, when the odds will be in his favour.'

'We'd better get your father to the doctor,' Law cut in. 'He looks real bad hurt. Leave me to worry about what I might or might not have to do. From what I've heard already, you've got rather more on your plate than you can handle. Go ahead and do what you have to and I'll be around to ease the way for you. We'll get your pa fixed up, and then we can relax and talk over your problems. I have business to handle around here so I can't take a job with you. But I'll see you through your present difficulties.'

'Help me get Pa out of the buggy. Doc Rouse's office is just past that alley.'

Law helped Ben Rutherford out of the buggy. The rancher seemed only half aware of his surroundings, and Law noted several bad bruises on the man's forehead and right temple that could only have been caused by a vicious pistol-whipping. He slid his left shoulder into Rutherford's right armpit, took his weight, and half-carried him across the sidewalk, preceded by Julie, who opened the door of the doctor's office and led the way inside.

Easing Rutherford into a chair, Law remained in the background while Julie spoke to the doctor's receptionist, a small, middle-aged lady who arose from her desk and came to examine the rancher.

'What on earth happened to Ben, Julie? Was he thrown from his horse? He should be in bed, not bumping around over half the countryside to get here. Doc would have come out to the Circle R if you'd sent for him.'

'Some Big G bullies showed up at the ranch this morning and did this to Pa,' Julie said. 'They told us to be off the ranch by sun-up tomorrow.'

Law moved to the window overlooking the street and glanced around. He could see Crowley, the deputy sheriff, talking to two riders who had just arrived in town. The riders came on along the street and Law watched them, noting their appearance. Both were heavily armed and had much about them that bespoke of their business. They were gun men, and looked to be on the prod as they reined up beside the buggy and dismounted to stand chatting beside it.

'Julie, come take a look at two riders outside,' Law said easily.

She came to his side and a gasp

escaped her as she glanced through the window.

'They're Big G riders. That's Hawk Bassell in the red shirt, and the other is Art Riley! They were out at our spread this morning with others, and Bassell was the one who beat up Pa.' Julie dropped her hand to the butt of her .38. 'I'll kill them for what they did to Pa!'

'I don't think so.' Law lifted her pistol from its holster and thrust it into his waistband. 'Stay in here with your father and I'll go out and see what's doing.'

He opened the door and went out to the sidewalk. Both men by the buggy turned to look at him. Bassell was big with plenty of flesh on his tall frame. He was wearing a pistol in a tied-down holster on his right thigh, and his hand dropped to the butt of the weapon as he gazed at Law. Riley was a medium-sized man, but broad in the shoulders, and powerfully set up.

'Bassell and Riley,' Law said, moving

to the edge of the sidewalk and looking down at the tough pair.

'Who in hell are you?' Bassell demanded. 'I ain't seen you around before. How'd you know us?'

'Julie Rutherford hired me about five minutes ago. She's in the doc's office with her father, and pointed you two out to me. I'm standing up for Circle R, so you're gonna have to deal with me in future. Now about that message you gave Ben Rutherford this morning, and the beating you handed out to him. What was it again? I'd like to hear it so there's no mistake.'

A silence ensued, and Law could tell by the expressions of both men that they were shocked by his confrontation. Riley began to edge away from Bassell, and Law drew his gun so fast that both men blinked in shock.

'Let's do this right,' Law said quietly. 'One at a time, get rid of your guns. Drop them in the dust. Then we'll talk. You first, Bassell.'

The gunman lifted his weapon clear

of its holster, using thumb and forefinger only, and dropped it without protest, his face stiff with rage, but the steady .45 in Law's hand discouraged resistance and he had the sense to obey. Not so Riley. The fingers of his right hand flexed and then were still.

'Nobody takes my gun off me,' Riley rasped.

'OK.' Law returned his Colt to its holster with a slick movement, and then remained still, his hand down at his side. 'It's your choice, Riley, so make your play.'

Riley's face underwent imperceptible changes of expression. He drew a deep breath and restrained it, and then his gun hand moved fast, dipping down and filling with his pistol. Law moved simultaneously. His Colt cleared greased leather and exploded deafeningly, the report echoing across the street, and a half-inch chunk of lead smacked dust from Riley's shirt front.

For a timeless instant, Riley stood immobile, his gun only half-drawn, his face proclaiming shock. Then he folded at the neck, waist and knees and sagged to the ground. Law stood motionless, his hard gaze upon Bassell as the raucous echoes of the deadly shot reverberated across the town.

'You got the same choice,' Law said quietly. 'Pick up your gun if you're so minded, and we'll start over.'

'Riley never had any sense,' Bassell said hoarsely. 'But me, I ain't drawing against you, mister.'

'Then get the hell out of here. Split the breeze out of town and don't come back. I'll kill you on sight if I set eyes on you again. Do you get the message or shall I repeat it?'

Bassell gazed into Law's eyes, and what he read there scared him off. He half-bent to pick up his gun but thought better of the action and straightened.

'Beat it,' Law rapped.

Bassell went to his horse, swung into the saddle and rode back the way he had come. Law watched him, saw him ignore Crowley, who was watching from the front of the hotel and shouted a question at him as he went by. Bassell did not look left or right, but rode fast for other parts. Crowley stared after him for a moment, and then turned to face Law. He came along the street at a half-run, pistol in hand.

Law watched the deputy. Crowley was not made for running, and was breathless by the time he reached Law. He halted, shoulders heaving, and the muzzle of his pistol was pointing downwards, as if he had forgotten that he was holding the weapon. He tried to speak but failed to do more than croak, and turned his attention to the inert Riley. He dropped to one knee, grasped the man's shirt front and endeavoured to shake some response from him.

'Stop that,' Law rapped. 'Can't you see he's dead?'

Crowley pushed himself erect. His heavy face was pasty, his eyes wide in shock. He lifted his pistol, and Law erupted into action. He blocked Crowley's gun with his left hand and slid his right foot forward half a pace as he whirled his shoulders and threw a solid right punch to the deputy's head. His knuckles landed on the side of the jaw and Crowley went over backwards like an uprooted tree to crash into the dust and lie still.

Law kicked Crowley's pistol away, sending it skittering through the dust. He looked around the street and saw several men watching in the background, but no one had the nerve to come out into the open. Law sighed and dropped to one knee beside Crowley. He used the same tactics Crowley had used on Riley, grasping the deputy's shirt front and shaking the man. Crowley groaned and his eyelids flickered. Law slapped Crowley's face several times, and the big deputy returned to his senses.

Law grinned as he stood up. Crowley scrambled to his feet and stood swaying, trying to regain his scattered wits. He dropped his right hand to his empty holster, and then saw his pistol lying several yards away. He rubbed his jaw and faced Law.

'What in hell did you hit me for?' he demanded. 'I could jug you for assaulting a law officer.'

'I could have shot you instead,' Law said. 'Would you have preferred that?' He put his hand on his gun butt. 'You're not gonna jail me, Crowley. I'm a special deputy marshal from Amarillo, sent in to sort out this trouble you've got because you can't or won't handle it yourself. So back off and leave me to do what I have to.'

He lapsed into silence and awaited Crowley's reaction, ready to further humiliate the deputy if he had to. He had taken a hand in the game that was being played. The cards had been dealt before his arrival, and he had no choice but to make the best of it.

2

Crowley stared at Law in shocked silence, his lips moving silently as he regained his scattered wits. His eyes showed that Law's blow had robbed him of his customary bluster, and he blinked rapidly several times and shook his head repeatedly in an effort to clear it.

'You're a deputy marshal?' he repeated dazedly. 'Have you got proof of that? And if you're a law man then why in hell did you hit me?'

'I thought you were about to make a bad mistake, like trying to shoot me,' Law replied. 'I stopped you from making a fool of yourself, Crowley. For that, you should be grateful. My only option was to shoot you.'

Crowley shook his head. Law's words did not register with him. He staggered as he picked up his pistol, and then thrust the weapon into its holster and came back to stare down at Riley's corpse.

'Did you see what happened here?' Law asked.

'I saw, but I didn't believe it. Riley was one of the fastest guns around, and you beat him like he had no hands.'

'Get his body moved off the street. I've got things to do now, but I'll come to the law office later and we'll talk. Where's the sheriff? His name is Lew Derry, so I was told. He does his law dealing from Spanish Creek, huh? How often does he come here?'

'Never. I run this town. I report to him once a month.'

Law gazed at Crowley, and again had a fleeting impression that he should know the man, and wondered if it was because of the star-shaped scar on Crowley's face, He resolved to check wanted posters as soon as he could.

'I've seen reports about you that don't make good reading, mister,' Law said 'You ain't been doing your duty properly. You better knuckle down to some real law dealing or you'll wind up out of a job.'

Crowley turned away, shaking his head in disbelief.

'I'll be in the law office if you want me,' he said over his shoulder.

'Do something about Riley's body,' Law rapped.

A rider was coming along the street as Law stepped on to the sidewalk. The newcomer reined in to the sidewalk and dismounted. He was tall and thin, dressed in a good brown store suit, and took a small leather bag from his saddle horn and made as if to go to the inert Riley.

'You'll be wasting your time, Doc,' Law said. 'He's ready for the undertaker.'

'Did you kill him?'

'Sure.' Law let his right hand drop to his gun butt. 'I'm in that line of business.'

'There are too many of your kind around here already.'

'I'm different from the general run.' Law smiled.

'You don't look like a man who is intent upon committing suicide. There's a big turnover in gun men around here. That's the Rutherford buggy, isn't it?'

'Julie is waiting in your office with her father.' Law explained what had happened at Circle R that morning, and the doctor tut tutted and hurried into his office.

Law glanced around the street. Townsfolk were coming into view now, edging towards the spot where Riley was lying. Shaking his head slowly, Law entered the doctor's office and motioned to Julie to join him. He led her outside as the doctor began an examination of Ben Rutherford, and stood with her on the sidewalk. She was badly shocked, and stood gazing narrow-eyed at Riley's corpse, until Law shook her gently.

'I suggest you stick around town for a few days,' he said firmly. 'That will give me time to look up the men you said were breaking the law out at your place. I'll visit Seth Geest at Big G and get his view of the rustling your outfit is supposed to be doing.'

'We never stole a cow in our lives!'

'Sure. I know. Don't worry about it. I'm a lawman and I don't listen to rumours. I look at the facts and act accordingly. But you've got to take care. You're my witness for what happened at your place this morning. I'll arrest all the men involved and then we'll get to the bottom of this trouble. I've studied a map of the county, and I reckon I can find my way around. Geest's ranch is out to the west, huh?'

'Sure. Take the trail out of town and just follow it. You'll pass our spread about ten miles out, and Big G is five miles on.' She paused, shaking her head. 'So you won't be working for Circle R?'

'I'll be working for you if you're innocent,' Law replied. 'But you've got to promise to stay out of trouble. Don't go fighting anyone around here. Leave the rough stuff to me.'

'I promise.' She nodded, her eyes still on the inert figure of Riley stretched out in the dust.

'Is there anything you can tell me about this business that will point me in the right direction? I don't want suspicions, only hard proof.'

'Arrest the whole outfit at Big G and there won't be any trouble left.'

'That will do for a start.' Law smiled. 'I hope your father will be OK. See you around.'

Law left her and walked along the sidewalk to the saloon. He needed a drink before collecting supplies, and wanted to be on the trail for Big G without delay. He attended to his needs, collected fresh provisions from the store, and was riding out of town ten minutes later.

He headed west, following the trail leading in that direction, and rode steadily through the hot afternoon.

Ten miles along the trail he spotted a

cluster of ranch buildings off to the right and turned aside to visit the spread. A small house was situated beside a meandering stream. There was a bunkhouse, a barn, a cook shack and a corral, but little else. He paused at the gate and looked around. The place seemed deserted, and he wondered about the Circle R crew.

He leaned down from his saddle to open the gate and, as he entered the yard, a rifle cracked and dust spurted up very close to the forefeet of his dun. He reined in and sat motionless astride his horse, looking around, and spotted a puff of gun smoke drifting away from a front window of the house, but no sign of movement. Then a voice called to him.

'Who are you and what do you want, mister? This is private property.'

'I've been hired by Julie Rutherford,' Law replied. 'Who are you?'

'Tim Arlott. There's only me and the cook, Dab Hamley, left on the place.'

There was movement at the front

door, and then a tall, thin man stepped out to the porch. He held a levelled rifle in his hands. Law rode across the yard, and caught a glimpse of sunlight glinting on the twin barrels of a shotgun protruding from a window in the cook shack to his left. He reined up in front of the porch and looked down at the cowpoke. Arlott was in his early thirties. He had a protruding jaw, red hair and a worried expression on his face.

'I'm Jed Law.' He explained what had happened in Buffalo Crossing and Arlon cursed silently.

'I knew I should have gone into town with them,' he said, shaking his head. 'But you can't argue with a girl. And you beat Riley to the draw? Heck, I wish I could have seen that.'

'Did you see Bassell and Doughty and the Big G riders come in here this morning and beat up Ben Rutherford?'

'I sure did. I would have taken my gun to them if they hadn't caught us flat-footed. But there's nothing I can do now except get myself killed. The rest of the outfit has quit cold. There's only me and the cook left, and I guess we'll be out of a job tomorrow. Geest means to take over this place and now no one can stop him.'

'Go into town if you do leave here, and wait for me to return. I'll need you as a witness against the Big G men who rode in this morning.'

'Do you mean to ride to Big G and take them on?' Arlott's eyes glinted. 'I'll ride with you. It's about time someone stuck up for Circle R.'

'You stay out of it and do like I say. You'd be helping the ranch better by giving evidence against the men I arrest.'

'I'd like to go along and see you arrest the likes of Doughty and Bassell. They're dyed-in-the-wool gunslingers and won't back down from anyone. You'll have to kill them.'

'Riley had the same attitude,' Law pointed out, and Arlott fell silent, shaking his head.

Footsteps sounded in the yard and

Law looked around at the short, fat, balding man who was coming towards them from the cook shack. He was carrying a double-barrelled shotgun in his right hand, and wore an off-white apron around his bulging waist. His wrinkled face was black with stubble and stained with suspicion. He looked ready to fight.

'What's going on?' he demanded. 'Anything I can do, Tim?'

'You could give me a meal before I ride on,' Law said.

Arlott introduced him to the cook, and Hamley's manner changed when he heard about Riley's death. He turned about and started back to the cook shack.

'Gimme about twenty minutes,' he called over his shoulder, 'and then come and get it.'

Law nodded. He glanced around, checking the approaches to the ranch, and stiffened when he saw dust hazing just beyond the corral.

'Something's moving out there,' he observed.

Arlott cocked his rifle instantly and called to the cook, who was halfway to his shack.

'Dab, there's something moving out there beyond the corral.'

Hamley paused to look around as a rifle cracked like a whip, throwing a string of flat echoes across the range. Hamley flung down his shotgun and pitched sideways. Arlott started running towards the cook, but Law grasped his left arm and pulled him to a halt.

'Get under cover,' he ordered, and turned and ran for the door of the ranch house as a volley of shots hammered and lead crackled around them.

Arlott cursed and sprang on to the porch. He was in the doorway of the house when a bullet struck him in the back. Law heard a cry, and turned to see the cowboy pitching forward on to his face on the threshold. He dragged Arlott into cover, looked into his face, and sighed when he saw the man was unconscious. He eased Arlott into a sitting position to examine him and found a bullet wound low in his left shoulder. He lowered Arlott back to the floor and turned to the nearest window to take a look outside.

Three riders were coming into the yard, moving around the corral off to the right. They were carrying weapons at the ready and moving cautiously, separating as they crossed the yard towards the house. One of them dismounted beside the inert body of Dab Hamley and dropped to one knee to examine the man. He straightened almost instantly and triggered his pistol twice, shooting the cook in the chest, and then grinned at his two intent companions as he waved them on. They came at a walk to the house, primed for trouble.

Law drew his pistol, incensed by the cold-blooded murder of the cook. He went to the door and stepped out to the porch, his pistol down at his side. His movement attracted the attention of the trio and they reined in to look at him.

'I'm working for Circle R,' Law called, his voice echoing in the uneasy silence that had settled over the yard. 'Work your guns, you killers.'

The trio jolted into action, lifting their weapons, and Law triggered his Colt, grimly satisfied as he fanned his hammer, his eyes narrowed against flaring gun smoke. A drum roll of shots blasted out in the silence, and only one of the trio managed to fire a shot before Law's slugs cut them down. He watched them tumbling out of their saddles. Two never moved again after they had hit the dust, and the third lay writhing in agony, like a snake that had been stepped on.

Law remained motionless for long moments, looking around, listening to the fading gun echoes. Then he methodically reloaded the used chambers in his pistol, and carried the weapon in his hand as he stepped down into the yard. He had shot to kill two of the men and aimed to wound one of them, and his boots raised little puffs of dust as he advanced upon them.

He spared no more than a glance at the two dead men, and dropped to one knee beside the man that had killed Hamley. He threw away the man's discarded pistol and looked down into a bearded face that was twisted in pain. Blood was showing on the man's right shoulder. Mean eyes peered up at him. The man tried to speak but only a groan emerged from his bloodied lips.

Law realized that his shot had struck lower than he had intended. The man was very seriously wounded.

'What's your name and why did you murder the cook?' Law asked.

'We came to take over the place and were told to leave no witnesses. Who in hell are you?'

'I'm asking the questions. Do you work for Big G?'

'Who else? You better get out of here fast, mister. More of the crew will be along shortly, and if you wanta live you better not be here when they show up.'

'What's your name?' Law repeated.

'Hap Jones.'

'And the other two?'

'Tom Ferris and Bill Bland.'

'Who gave you the order to ride in and kill the men here?'

'Go ask the boss at Big G.' Jones lapsed into unconsciousness.

Law got to his feet and went into the house to check on Arlott. He shook his head when he found the cowboy was dead, and went out to his horse, appalled by the cold-blooded murders, but now he knew exactly what he was up against. He went back to Hap Jones and saw that he, too, had died, and then mounted and rode out, following the tracks left by the three killers as they came in across the undulating range. The afternoon was well past, the fiery orb of the sun now close to the western horizon. He rode alertly, ready for trouble, and had no problems following the tracks of the three riders.

When he topped a rise and saw a

large ranch in the near distance he rode back across the skyline and dismounted. Moving up again, he flattened himself and lay studying the ranch. Several men were in evidence in the yard, some carrying rifles, and they looked as if they were prepared for trouble. Law watched with glinting eyes. He was here to give them what they were expecting, and there was no mercy in his mind.

He could see that the tracks of the murderous trio had come out of the ranch, and looked around for a covered approach to the huddle of stark buildings clustered around a narrow creek. The sun was slipping behind the horizon as he began to circle, staying in dead ground to avoid being seen, and heavy shadows lay across the land as he dismounted well to the rear of the ranch house and tethered the dun.

Carrying his rifle in his left hand, he went forward through the growing darkness towards the house, moving carefully, and reached the back wall of the wooden building without seeing anyone. He stood in the darkness, listening intently. Yellow lantern light was coming from the kitchen and he eased along the wall until he could peer through a small window. An old man wearing a white apron was busy inside, cooking supper, and Law was reminded that he had not eaten all day.

He moved on, circling the house until he reached a front corner, and heard voices as he peered around it to look across the shadowed porch. Two men were seated on chairs on the porch, and Law listened intently.

'You'll take some of the crew to Circle R in the morning and move in, Tog,' one of the men said. 'Jones and his pards will have cleaned up over there by then. When you get there you'll hold the place against all-comers.'

'Who do you reckon can give us trouble?' the other demanded, laughing harshly. 'You got Crowley on your side, Seth, and no one around town will be interested in what happens to the Rutherfords. You've branded them as rustlers, and folks will be pleased to see them go.'

'While Ben Rutherford is alive he'll make trouble, and that daughter of his is a wildcat. She ain't never gonna quit. I reckon she'll have to be done away before we can relax. I'm not running this business alone, remember. I've got partners, although I don't like them.'

'You got plenty of men around here who will do for the gal for a few dollars, and her father, too, if you've a mind to be done with them.'

'Tomorrow will be soon enough to think about that. Come on, let's go in and eat. Supper should be ready by now. I want you riding out of here before the sun shows tomorrow.'

Both men arose and moved to the door of the house. They entered and their voices were lost to Law, who stood in the shadows considering what he had overheard. He went around to the back of the house again and peered through the kitchen window. Both men were now seated at a table and the cook was serving them hot food.

Law studied the older man, whom he took to be Seth Geest, a big raw-boned individual, wide-shouldered and powerful. Geest had removed his Stetson, revealing a shock of unruly black hair. His harshly set face had narrowed, spiteful eyes, and his mouth was mean, his lips thin and tight against his teeth.

The younger man, Tog, was in his thirties, thin like a bean pole, with narrow shoulders and fair hair. He was wearing twin six-shooters on crossed gunbelts, and had not removed them before sitting down at the table.

The top half of the window was open slightly, and Law could hear the mumble of their voices as the two men ate their meal, but was unable to make out what was being said. He waited patiently, and some twenty minutes had passed when the inner door to the kitchen was thrust open and a young man entered who was tall and well set up, with broad shoulders and a powerful body. Law figured the new-comer looked a lot like Seth Geest, and his first words confirmed the suspicion.

'Pa, have you heard the news? There was hell to pay in town. Riley was shot dead, beaten to the draw by a stranger who rode in, and Bassell showed yeller and left his gun in the dust and headed out. I always said he was a snake. Didn't he tell you about it?'

'Simmer down, Chance, and give it to me straight. What are you running on about?' Seth Geest dropped his knife and fork and leaned back in his chair, his mean eyes studying his son's face. 'Bassell ain't showed up since I sent him to town with Riley to watch the Rutherfords. Who's the stranger that showed up? Is it the State deputy Crowley said the sheriff mentioned last week?'

'I don't know who he is. He'd ridden out by the time I got there. I saw Leroy Cooper in town and he told me the stranger got between him and Julie Rutherford. Leroy reached for his gun and the stranger outdrew him by a mile. Leroy reckoned he'd never seen anyone draw faster. The whole town is talking about it.'

'Do you want me to handle it, Seth?' Tog Doughty demanded.

'If he's a deputy marshal then we've gotta walk careful around him,' Geest mused. 'We've got the situation here in a critical state right now, and I want it settled before anyone from outside comes sticking his nose in. If this Johnny-come-lately is a marshal then he'd better disappear while he's on the range, not in town. We wouldn't want any witnesses. You say he left town, Chance?'

'Yeah. He pulled out, and rode in this direction. He could be out there right now, watching the spread and weighing up the situation.

'Get out there and take a look round, Tog,' Geest said instantly. 'In the morning you better search the area for tracks. If there is a lawman then I want him pronto, and face down across his saddle. You got that?'

'Sure thing, boss.' Doughty pushed himself to his feet and hitched up his gunbelts, grinning as he went to the door. 'I'll find out just how fast this stranger is. I never found anyone faster than me. I could outshade Riley with no trouble at all.'

'You'll need to be a lot faster than that,' Chance Geest warned. 'Riley found himself out of his class.'

Law smiled in the darkness and slipped away from the window. He went around to the front corner of the house and waited for Doughty to appear on the porch. The gunman stepped down into the yard and started across to the bunkhouse. Law prepared to follow, but at that instant he heard a slight sound at his back, as of boot leather scraping against the ground. He tensed, but before he could act the muzzle of a pistol bored against his spine and a harsh voice challenged him.

'Freeze, mister, or I'll split your spine. Who in hell are you, sneaking around here in the dark?'

3

'Take it easy,' Law said instantly. 'I'm getting some air. I've just finished supper with Geest and Doughty. I rode in from town thirty minutes ago with news of the shooting there.'

'What shooting?' The muzzle of the gun at Law's back dug a little harder against his spine.

'Riley was shot dead this afternoon, beaten in an even break.'

'The hell you say! Who beat him?'

'Some stranger showed up and hired himself out to the Rutherfords. He braced Bassell and Riley. Bassell backed down but Riley attempted to draw and came second. Bassell tossed his gun into the dust and rode out fast. He ain't been seen since.'

'Jeez! What did Seth say about that?'

'He told Doughty to take care of it.'

Law felt the gun muzzle ease its

pressure against his spine and drew a deep breath. When he heard the rasp of the pistol being returned to its holster he whirled on the balls of his feet, his left hand lifting to grasp the guard's shirt front while his right fist came up and over in a powerful hook. His knuckles slammed against a solid chin. There was a gasp and the guard began to fold at the knees. Law caught and lowered him to the ground.

He sneaked the man's pistol out of its holster and slammed the barrel against his skull. He straightened and looked around quickly, probing the shadows, trying to judge if Doughty had caught any sound of the incident. He exhaled his pent-up breath silently when he saw Doughty in the act of entering the bunkhouse fifty yards away, the open door throwing a great shaft of yellow light across the coral, and he did not move until the bunkhouse door closed behind the gunman.

Considering the situation, he bent and lifted the unconscious man across his shoulder and then started away from the house before cutting away to where he had left his horse in concealment. He took a pair of handcuffs from his saddle-bag, snapped a cuff around the man's right wrist, and locked the other cuff around a thick branch of a fallen tree. He used the man's neckerchief as a gag, and the man was regaining his senses by the time Law was ready to return to the house.

'If I hear any noise from you I'll come back and silence you permanent,' Law warned. 'Have you got that?'

His prisoner grunted, and Law returned to the ranch house. He peered in at the kitchen window once more, but Seth Geest had finished his supper and was gone. Chance Geest was eating, and the old cook was clearing away. Law needed a hot meal, but fought down his hunger. He moved around the perimeter of the house, checking each lighted room as he came to it.

He saw Seth Geest in his office, seated at a desk, poring over a thick ledger. Law wanted to take Geest prisoner, but he would need a horse for the crooked rancher, so he moved away from the house to check on the barn, away behind the bunkhouse. Darkness covered his movements, but prevented him from looking around properly.

He entered the barn and found two horses in a stall inside. He struck a match and looked around quickly before the tiny flame died, and saw a saddle and bridle on the top rail of the stall. He selected a big black horse that looked as if it belonged to someone of the rancher's stature, prepared it for travel, and then led the high-spirited animal out of the back door of the barn and walked it wide of the house, moving slowly to avoid making noise, and finally reached the spot where his dun was tethered. He tied the black beside his mount.

His prisoner was lying silent and still where he had been left, and Law checked him before returning to the house. He went straight to the front door, drew his pistol, and entered silently. Opening the door of Geest's office, he confronted the rancher with levelled gun, and Geest froze behind the desk, his heavy features expressing shock.

'Don't make a sound and you might make it through the night,' Law told him. 'I'm the deputy marshal your son told you about, and I'm gonna take you into town and put you in jail. You're under arrest, Geest, and I better tell you that in the seven years I've been doing this job I've never lost a prisoner, but I've killed three men who reckoned to get away from me.'

'What in hell are you talking about?' Geest shook his head. 'You can't arrest me. I haven't broken any laws.'

'I overheard your conversation with Doughty on the porch and when you were eating your supper. You admitted sending three men to Circle R to take it over, and named Hap Jones as one of them. I was at Circle R when Jones murdered the cook in cold blood, and that is the charge I'm gonna hold you on. Now we're walking out of here, and if you've got any sense you'll stay quiet.'

'I ain't goin' anywhere with you,' Geest rasped, his eyes glittering with anger. 'You can't come in here and treat me like this.'

'You can complain to Crowley when we get to town. Get up and walk or I'll tote you out unconscious. It's all the same to me.'

Geest got to his feet and lifted his hands away from his waist. Law could see that the rancher was not armed, but moved in close to search the man. He expected Geest to try and overpower him, but Geest refrained from action. They left the house without incident and walked away through the darkness to where the horses were waiting. Law released the man he had taken prisoner, and Geest complained in a low tone as they mounted. Law kept his pistol in his hand as they departed.

They walked their horses for half a mile before Law judged that they could quicken the pace, and then they proceeded at a mile-eating lope. The night was mysterious around them, silent and uncertain with faint starlight and a thin crescent moon high and remote. They eventually saw the lights of Buffalo Crossing, and Law judged the time to be around midnight.

The town was mainly dark, but music was still sounding from the big saloon along the street. A light was showing in the law office, and Law reined in before it and stepped down from his saddle. Geest dismounted, and seemed to lose his balance as he stepped away from his horse. The next instant he launched himself at Law in a furious attack.

Law had been expecting a last-ditch move and sidestepped the rush. His right fist flew in a tight arc and smacked against Geest's chin. The rancher went down like a pole-axed steer and lay still. Law crossed the sidewalk to the door of the office. Thrusting it open, he looked inside and saw Crowley seated behind a desk, reading a newspaper. Law's nose twitched; the place smelled of cabbage.

'Come and give me a hand,' he said when Crowley looked up at him.

Crowley came to the door as Law went outside. The big deputy helped raise Geest out of the dust and carry him into the office, where they stretched him out on the floor. When lantern light fell upon Geest's pallid face, Crowley uttered a curse.

'Seth Geest!' he exclaimed. 'How did you get him away from his crew?'

'It was not a problem.' Law smiled. 'I reckon it will be a lot harder to keep him behind bars, but that is where you come in, Crowley. Out at Big G I heard Tog Doughty say that you were in Geest's pocket.'

'What the hell! I ain't nothing but a lawman.'

'I don't want to know anything but what your plans are from now on,' Law rapped. 'If you work with me then I'll hold you responsible for what you do, and you better not put a foot wrong. If Geest escapes from here then you'll face the music, and I'll hunt you down if I have to. So you got a choice. Quit your job now if you feel you can't carry out your duties as a deputy, or stand with me and go all the way.'

'I told you. I'm a lawman. If anyone thinks he can use me for his own ends then he's got a nasty surprise coming.'

Crowley bent over the stirring Geest, grasped the man's collar, and dragged him upright, using brute strength. Geest sagged in the deputy's grip and Crowley shook him.

'Wake up, Geest,' he rasped. 'You can sleep later.'

'Prop him up in a chair. I want to talk to him,' Law said.

Geest opened his eyes fully and looked around. He was dazed, but angry, and his mean eyes glittered as he regarded Law.

'You've made a big mistake, throwing your weight around,' he said at length.

'The law don't amount to anything in this county.'

'It might have looked like that before I arrived,' Law countered, 'but all that has changed now I'm running things, and I don't expect any trouble righting the wrongs that have been done. Over the next few days we'll find out what's been going on, and already I got enough to hold you on while I investigate. It looks like there'll be some pretty big charges settling on you, and your best bet is to level with me. Tell me the names of your partners and you might be able to help yourself.'

'You got nothing on me,' Geest said stolidly. 'And you'll find that out pretty damn quick when you try to get witnesses.' He laughed and shook his head. 'I'm waiting to see that. You ain't got a leg to stand on. Folks won't talk to you.'

'Lock him in a cell, Crowley,' Law said. 'We'll give him time to think over his position. I expect him to sing a different tune come morning.'

Crowley picked up a bunch of keys and led the way into the cell block. Law stood by while Geest was locked in a cell. He was feeling the effects of a long day with no food, and stiffened his shoulders as he led the way back into the front office.

'Are you on duty all night?' he asked Crowley.

'I shall be now, with a prisoner in the cells,' Crowley replied. 'You don't have to worry. Geest will still be behind bars tomorrow.'

'I need to eat. Can I get food at this time of the night?'

'Talk to Joe Mason in the saloon. He'll rustle up some grub for you. The Bull's Head will be open another hour at least.'

'I'll come back here in an hour and take over from you,' Law decided. 'Stay alert. I don't know when Geest will be missed from his ranch, but the town will be the first place anyone comes looking for him.'

He left the office and rode to the

livery barn. After taking care of his horse he walked along the street carrying his saddle-bags and rifle, and peered over the batwings into the saloon, blinking in the strong lamplight. There were at least a dozen men inside despite the lateness of the hour, and he saw Leroy Cooper sitting in on a poker game at a corner table. He walked to the bar and laid his saddle-bags and rifle on the polished woodwork.

The 'tender came towards him, a tall, thin man with sparse black hair soaked in grease and lying flat to his head. He was middle-aged, his face lined, his eyes ageless.

'Howdy,' he greeted. 'You're late riding in, stranger. What can I get you? We'll be closing in about an hour.'

'How about some food? I ain't eaten since breakfast. Anything will do at a pinch.'

'Sure. My wife will throw something together for you. She ain't gone to bed yet. Gimme a few minutes, huh? Would you like a drink while you're waiting?'

'Beer,' Law answered.

He looked around the saloon more closely and noted that Leroy Cooper was watching him from across the room while talking to the three men sharing his table. Law smiled to himself. Leroy was probably enthusing about the fast draw that had shocked him in front of Julie Rutherford that afternoon. Thinking of the girl, Law wondered how her father was doing, and then spotted Doc Rouse sitting at a table near the far end of the bar with two men who had the unmistakable look of prominent citizens about them.

Both the doctor's companions were dressed in black broadcloth. One was large, maybe sixty years of age, overweight, with a keen gaze and long fair hair. His fleshy face was not tanned, as if he spent most of his working hours out of the sun, and he was smoking a cigar while talking forcefully to the doctor. The other man was smaller, weasel-faced, in his thirties, his gaze darting constantly around the saloon but not resting anywhere. He looked at Law, caught his gaze, and looked away again immediately.

Law left the bar and walked to the table where Doc Rouse was sitting, and his presence cut off their conversation. The three men gazed up at him.

'What happened to Ben Rutherford, Doc?' Law asked. 'Was he badly hurt? He didn't look too good this afternoon.'

'I think he'll be all right,' Rouse replied. 'He's in bed in the hotel, and I'll be checking up on him again tomorrow. Julie was looking for you earlier. She wanted to see you about some problem or other. You are working for Circle R, aren't you?'

'I'm looking after their interests at the moment,' Law glanced at the doctor's two companions, who were regarding him with suspicion. 'Who are your friends, Doc?'

'This is Grat Kibbee,' Rouse said instantly, indicating the bigger man. 'He runs the bank in town. And this is Parker Strutt, the local attorney-at-law.'

'I was just saying to Doc that you must be some kind of a lawman,' Kibbee said in a booming tone. 'You were seen half-carrying someone into the law office a short time ago, aided by our estimable deputy sheriff, Scar Crowley.'

'I don't suppose much goes unnoticed in this town,' Law observed.

He turned away to return to his saddlebags and rifle, and Leroy Cooper left his table and came to him as he drank his beer.

'I'd like a word,' Leroy said.

Law noted that the man was not openly wearing a gun but there was a tell-tale bulge in his left armpit.

'OK,' he said. 'What's on your mind?'

'About this afternoon. I was out of line. I've bent over backwards trying to be friendly with Julie but she didn't want to know. Now she's in serious trouble, and I kind of lost my head when you stepped in and she hired you just like that. I had no intention of drawing against you. I'm not in that line of business, and when I heard what you did to Riley I reckoned you let me off light. I'm thankful for that.'

'What do you do around here?' Law countered.

'My pa owns Double C.'

'And you and Chance Geest are sidekicks, huh? Does your spread have any trouble with rustlers?'

'Nope. We can take care of ourselves.'

'And Big G. Do they have any trouble?'

'Only from Circle R. But nobody stands up to Seth Geest.'

'I wonder why that is. Geest didn't seem so tough when I invited him to see the inside of the jail.'

'You got him in jail?' Cooper's eyes gleamed for a moment, and a fleeting smile touched his lips but vanished before registering.

'He is behind bars right now, and I reckon it'll be a long time before he comes out.'

'That sounds good for Circle R, but jailing Geest is one thing; keeping him behind bars is another. Are you a lawman?'

'That's my business.' Law held Cooper's gaze and the man shook his head and turned away.

Law finished his beer as he watched Cooper going back to his table. Joe Mason appeared from a room out back and came along the bar.

'Food will be ready in about ten minutes,' he called. 'You can eat in the kitchen, if you want.'

'Sure. I'm so hungry I could eat standing on my head right now.'

'Have another beer while you're waiting. It comes free with your meal.'

'Thanks.' Law drank from the brimming glass that slid before him. He heard a commotion at the table where Cooper was seated, and glanced across the room.

One of the three men with Cooper was struggling to get to his feet and Leroy was holding him down with a big hand twisted in the man's shirt front.

'Cut it out, Boyce,' Cooper said. 'I

told you he killed Riley from an even break so you wouldn't have a snowball's chance in hell of beating him. He pulled his gun on me, and was prodding my belly with his muzzle before I'd half-drawn. That's how fast he is. Get wise, why don't you?'

'If he's got my boss in jail then I've gotta do something about it,' Boyce said. 'Turn me loose, damn you!'

Law walked across the room and paused before the table. Boyce ceased his struggles and peered blearily at him.

'Is it right you've jailed Seth Geest?' he demanded.

'You'd better find some place to sleep it off or you'll find yourself sharing Geest's cell,' Law replied.

Boyce renewed his struggling and managed to get his right arm free of Cooper's grasp. He slapped leather immediately, and then froze when he found himself staring into the muzzle of Law's gun. His mouth gaped in surprise and his eyes widened as he lifted his hand away from his hardware.

'Do you want to make a fresh start?' Law asked. 'You might get lucky next time. That wasn't my fastest draw. I get a mite tired this time of the night.'

'It's the fastest I've seen,' Cooper said. 'You're in a class of your own. You'd better behave, Boyce, or we'll have to bury you.'

'Get him out of here,' Law directed. 'I don't wanta set eyes on him again tonight or there will be trouble. I'm about to have a meal, and I don't wanta be bothered until I'm through in here. Have you got that?'

'We'll take care of it,' Cooper said.

He dragged Boyce towards the batwings, and Law watched them depart. He finished his drink, picked up his saddle-bags and rifle and followed Mason into the back room. The smell of cooking food hit him in the pit of the stomach as he sat down at a table, and he thanked Mason's wife profusely when she set a big meal before him.

Law ate quickly from habit, but even so, he was only halfway through the meal when the window in the wall overlooking the alley was broken and a gun muzzle came into view. Law hurled himself off the chair to his left, and his pistol was in his right hand before his shoulder hit the floor. He heard the quick blast of a gun, and hot lead splattered the area where he had been seated.

He triggered his Colt rapidly, sending three shots in the general direction of the window, and gun smoke stung his nostrils as he got to his knees, gun ready. But his attacker had gone, and he arose slowly, his ears ringing from the heavy gun blasts.

Joe Mason came into the room carrying a shotgun, his face pale, shock staring out of his eyes. Law went to the broken window and tried to look outside but could see nothing. There was a door beside the window and he opened it and looked out cautiously, but, as he suspected, the alley was deserted.

Cooper and Boyce would have

known he was about to have a meal in the kitchen, Law thought, and Boyce had been eager to confront him. He sighed regretfully because he had not finished his meal, but duty came before personal needs.

'Have you got any idea where Cooper would put Boyce down to sleep?' he asked Mason, who was standing in the doorway watching him.

'Were you taken in by Boyce acting drunk?' Mason countered. 'He was sober as a judge when you walked into the saloon. Him and his pards were playing poker, not drinking hard.'

'So it was a set-up!' Law reloaded the empty chambers in his pistol and slid the weapon back into its holster. 'I'll settle up with you later,' he said, and departed quickly by the alley door to walk to the main street.

He walked along the street towards the livery stable, and was approaching the big barn, which had a single lantern burning over the open doorway, when four riders emerged from its dark interior and rode straight at him, yelling like Indians and waving pistols. Gunfire blasted, but it was Law who fired first. He went to ground triggering his pistol, and rolled several times to put his attackers off their aim. His first shot took the foremost rider in the chest and his second downed the horse of the nearest rider, which crashed into the dust only feet from him, its rider taking a heavy fall and lying still.

The other two riders galloped by, twisting in their saddles to maintain their fire at him, and Law felt the fiery rake of a speeding bullet across the top of his right shoulder. He pushed himself up on one knee and sent two shots after his assailants. One rider swayed in his saddle and almost fell off the horse, but managed to retrieve his balance and galloped away along the street. Law remained motionless, gun uplifted, until the sound of hoofs faded and silence returned.

He turned his attention to the two downed riders. The man lying almost within an arm's length of him was Boyce, and Law could see that he was dead, his neck twisted awkwardly. He went to the second man and found him dead also, a bullet through the centre of his chest. It was not Leroy Cooper, and Law promised himself a confrontation with Cooper in the near future.

Feet sounded from along the street and Law turned to see a group of men coming towards him from the saloon, led by Joe Mason, who was still holding his shotgun. They came up and stood gazing at the prostrate men. Doc Rouse, who was among them, bent to examine both.

'Did anyone see where those two riders went?' Law asked. 'I think Leroy Cooper was one of them.'

'They headed straight out of town,' Mason said. 'And if they've got any sense they'll keep going and never come back.'

Law reloaded his pistol and holstered it. His right shoulder was painful, and he examined the area with his fingers, locating blood, but the wound seemed to be minor, and he refused treatment when Doc Rouse approached him.

'It's nothing,' he said. 'I'll see you later if it troubles me. I've got things to do right now.'

He went back along the street, intent on checking out the jail, but Julie Rutherford appeared in the doorway of the hotel as he reached it, and he paused when she called to him.

'What was all that shooting about?' she demanded.

'Nothing for you to worry about,' he replied. 'I was just tidying up some loose ends. I'll come and talk to you tomorrow, but there's one thing I'd like you to tell me, if you can? Have you any idea who killed your brother?'

'Who else but Seth Geest?' she demanded. 'And if Geest didn't do it himself then he paid someone to kill Dave.'

'So you don't know,' he observed. 'Don't worry about it. I'll see you tomorrow.'

He went on until he reached the law office and was surprised to find Crowley standing in the doorway, gun in hand. He pushed past the deputy to enter the office, and halted abruptly as Crowley jabbed him in the back with the muzzle of his pistol.

'I got you dead to rights,' Crowley said thickly, snaking Law's pistol from its holster. 'I got no choice in this. I know which side my bread is buttered so I got to go along with Seth Geest. I turned him loose, and now I'm gonna put you out of it, mister.'

4

Law paused for a split second, shocked by Crowley's action, and then he whirled to his left and spun around, his left elbow swinging out and catching the gun in Crowley's hand, forcing the muzzle away from his body. Crowley fired, but his muzzle was deflected and the bullet bored through the door between the office and the cells. Law seized Crowley's gun hand and twisted the smoking pistol out of the man's grasp. He struck Crowley with the gun, using a backhanded blow, and Crowley dropped to his knees.

Law holstered the pistol and grasped Crowley's shoulders, hauling the big man to his feet. He hit the deputy on the jaw with his right fist, and then let him fall to the floor. Crowley rolled on to his back and lay groaning. Law straightened and cuffed back his Stetson.

Picking up the cell keys, Law grasped Crowley by the scruff of the neck, dragged him into the cell block and locked him in a cell. He stood waiting for the big deputy to regain his senses. Crowley groaned several times before lifting a hand to his forehead, and then opened his eyes and looked around dazedly. When he saw Law watching him through the bars of the cell door he pushed himself to his ·feet and sank down on a corner of the bunk, holding his head in his hands, his elbows propped on his knees.

'You made a real mess of that, Crowley,' Law said. 'Your best bet now is to tell me what's been going on around here and how you're involved. If you're not into it too deeply then you might be able to get out of it without too much trouble, but Dave Rutherford was murdered, and someone is gonna hang for that.'

'I don't know anything about that.' Crowley spoke in a hoarse tone, his fleshy face beaded with sweat. He shook his head obdurately. 'I got nothing to say to you. Seth Geest will come back here with his whole outfit tomorrow, and they'll turn me loose when they've done with you.'

'Don't hold your breath waiting for it to happen,' Law replied. 'Think about it until morning. You might feel differently about talking when you've had time to consider your position. I got a feeling I read your description on a dodger but I can't remember where at the moment.'

He went back into the front office and closed the street door, turning the big key in the lock. He sat down at the desk and leaned back in the chair, thinking about the situation. Crowley was a slender lead to what was going on, but he would not bank on the crooked deputy talking in the morning. If he rearrested Seth Geest, the event might loosen Crowley's tongue, but he feared it would not be so easy to take Geest a second time.

And Geest was not solely responsible for the trouble boiling over in the county. The rancher had admitted to having partners. But Law knew he had to find his own proof, and fancied that he was well on the way to making a break-through — or had been until Crowley turned against the law.

There was a large-scale map of Lomas County on the wall behind the desk and Law arose to study it. He pin-pointed Circle R, and Big G five miles along the trail west, and then found Double C off to the north some eight miles farther on from Big G. He wondered if Leroy Cooper had headed for his father's ranch, and realized that he should concentrate on picking up Leroy instead of going back to Big G for Seth Geest.

He turned abruptly and left the office to return to the saloon. The crowd that had gathered around the bodies in front of the stable had returned to the saloon for drinks, and were talking about the shooting that had taken place. Silence fell when Law pushed through the batwings, and many suspicious gazes were cast in his direction. Doc Rouse and his two companions, Kibbee and Strutt, were seated at a table, drinking and discussing the fight, and Rouse signalled for Law to join them.

'Does the town employ a night jailer?' Law asked when he stood before them.

'Not since Crowley became the deputy here,' Rouse said. 'The first thing you should do is get rid of Crowley.'

'I've arrested him. That's why I need someone to run the jail while I'm out of town. And I need a man to ride to Spanish Creek with a message for the sheriff.'

'You'd better talk to Deke Manson. He runs the hotel, and is the town mayor. He'll help you out.' Rouse leaned his elbows on the table and gazed at Law with expressionless eyes. 'Exactly what is your job, and what's your name?'

'I'm Jed Law, a State deputy marshal.' Law pulled aside the lapel of his vest and revealed his shield-shaped silver-coloured badge which glinted in the lamp light. It was plain, with the words STATE DEPUTY MARSHAL on it. 'I have more power than a county sheriff, and I can call upon anyone to help me perform my duty.'

He turned away, aware that Parker Strutt was gazing at him much like a rabbit looking at a weasel about to pounce. The attorney-at-law's gaze was unblinking, regarding Law intently, but slid away whenever Law tried to meet his gaze. Strutt's face was sweaty and he looked nervous.

'I'd better have a word with Manson,' Law said in departing, and was conscious of the silence that reigned as he crossed to the batwings. He went along to the hotel and found a small, bald-headed, middle-aged man behind a reception desk that was almost hidden under the stairs that led to the upper storey.

'Do you want a room?' the man demanded.

'No. I want to talk to Manson. Is he around?'

'Not at this time of the night he ain't. You better come back in the morning, after eight. I wouldn't wake Manson now if there was an earthquake.'

'Does he sleep in the hotel?'

'Sure does.'

'Which room?'

'I can't tell you that.'

Law reached across the desk, grasped the man by his shirt front, and hauled him close until their faces were only a few inches apart.

'This is the wrong time of day to stall me,' he grated. 'I'm a lawman, and you're obstructing me in my lawful duty. Do you want to spend the night in jail?'

'No, sir! I'll fetch Mr Manson immediately.' The clerk hurried away when Law released him, and ascended the stairs.

Law waited patiently. Minutes passed,

and then a big man descended the stairs, his fleshy face set in grim lines. He was wearing a hastily donned dressing-gown and his hair was uncombed.

'What's so important that it couldn't wait until morning?' he demanded. 'Do you know what the time is?'

'My job is more important than your sleep,' Law replied. 'Sorry to drag you out of bed but I need a night jailer, and a rider to carry a message to Sheriff Derry in Spanish Creek. You're the town mayor, and you can get things moving for me. I need to be in a certain place by sun up, and I won't be able to do that if I have to wait around for you.'

'Bill Baylin worked as night jailer until Crowley took over as deputy sheriff in the town. Baylin won't work with Crowley.'

'He won't have to. Crowley is behind bars. He's finished as a deputy.'

'The hell you say!' Manson perked up at the news, and smiled. 'Baylin will love to run the jail with Crowley in the cells. I'll go tell Baylin to report to you at once. And I know just the man to take your message to Sheriff Derry. Give me a few minutes and you'll have your help.'

'I'll be in the law office.' Law turned away.

He returned to the jail and sat at the desk considering his plans. Presently the sound of approaching boots rapped the sidewalk and then the street door was thrust open. A tall, thin man appeared, blinking his eyes in the lamplight. He was in his early thirties and wore a brown store suit. A double-barrelled Greener 12 gauge shotgun was tucked under his right arm.

'Marshal Law?' he came into the office and closed the door. 'I'm Bill Baylin. You need a night jailer.'

'Glad to know you, Bill. Can you take over as of now?'

'I sure can.' Baylin grinned. 'Is it true you've jailed Crowley?'

'Come and take a look at him.' Law picked up the keys and led the way into the cell block, saying, 'He turned Seth Geest loose after I'd arrested him, and then disarmed me. I think he was planning to kill me.'

'And finished up the wrong side of the bars, huh? That says a lot for your law dealing, Marshal. I'm gonna enjoy coming back here to work.'

Crowley looked up at them as they paused in front of his cell door.

'I'm glad to see you where you belong, Crowley,' Baylin said. 'It ain't before time, either. I always knew you were a wrong 'un.'

Crowley cursed and turned his face away from the door, complaining about the lateness of the hour. Law led the way back into the office, locked the door to the cell block, and handed the keys to Baylin, who grinned and sat down at the desk.

'I'll be riding out soon,' Law said, 'and I won't be back until noon tomorrow at the earliest. I'm waiting for a messenger who will ride to Spanish Creek and warn the sheriff that he needs another deputy here. Until a new man arrives, we're going to be shorthanded.'

'I'll fill in until someone arrives,' Baylin said. 'You can leave this side of the business to me.'

Law nodded. They chatted together until the office door opened and a man entered.

'Howdy, Marshal. I'm Jeff Turner. Deke Manson told me you want someone to ride to Spanish Creek with a message for the sheriff. Gimme the word and I'll split the breeze.'

'Crowley is in jail and I want another deputy sheriff in here to run things,' Law said.

'Is that it?' Turner nodded. 'OK. I'm on my way.'

He departed, and Law heaved a sigh. He took his leave and went to the stable for his dun, and minutes later he was riding back along the street on his way out of town. A man called to him as he was passing the hotel and he turned aside and reined in, surprised to see Doc Rouse.

'I was about to come to the law office for you,' Rouse said. 'I decided to check on Ben Rutherford before turning in, and he ain't here. The clerk told me Julie fetched her buggy, loaded Ben into it, and headed out to Circle R. You'd better do something about her, Marshal. It ain't fit for her to be out on the range alone, and Ben is in no state to be out of bed.'

'Thanks.' Law swung his horse instantly and spurred the animal along the street, his thoughts harsh as he considered Julie. She was a law unto herself, and if he did not make her pull in her horns she could give him more trouble than all the bad men together.

He travelled as fast as he dared in the darkness, following the trail that led to Circle R, and caught up with the buggy two miles out of town, almost riding into the back of the vehicle, which Julie had halted when she heard the sound of his approach.

'Declare yourself,' the girl cried in a

high-pitched tone. 'I've got a gun on you.'

'I'm Marshal Law. I need to talk to you.' He reined in beside the buggy. Julie was shapeless in the night, her face a pale blur in the starlight. Ben Rutherford was slumped in the seat beside her, evidently asleep. 'What are you doing out here?' he demanded. 'Are you trying to kill your father? He should be in bed. Doc Rouse told you what to do.'

'We'll be safer out at the ranch. I was not happy sitting around town.'

'I didn't tell you earlier, but the two men you left at the ranch are both dead.' He related the incident, and heard a groan of anguish escape her. 'So you'd better turn around and head back to the hotel. You'll be a heap safer there than at the ranch.'

'There's no end to it,' she said quietly. 'It's hopeless trying to carry on. I'll go back to town. What are you going to do?'

'When I'm certain I don't have to

worry about what you might do I'll get on with my job. I want to be at your ranch when the sun comes up. Now turn around and head back to the hotel, and stay there until I show up around town again.'

She turned the buggy in silence and set off back along the trail. Law sat his dun listening to the receding sounds of her departure, and when full silence returned he shook his reins to continue towards Circle R. The night around him was dark and mysterious, and nothing moved in the surrounding shadows.

He did not ride into the ranch when he reached it. The silence was intense, and he dismounted out of earshot of the buildings and made camp to rest until dawn. He rolled himself in his blanket but did not sleep, and was up and ready to ride when the first glimmer of sunlight strayed over the eastern horizon to herald the approach of a new day.

The Circle R ranch was silent and

still. Law moved into a spot from which he could study the buildings, and used his field glasses to examine every inch of the front yard. His gaze lingered on the bodies stretched out in the dust, and his expression was grim as he waited in cover.

Seth Geest had ordered Tog Doughty to take over the ranch at daybreak, and Law waited patiently for the gunman to arrive with his hard cases. The sun was well above the skyline when he heard hoofs approaching, and then two riders appeared on the trail and rode into the ranch yard. They spurred forward when they saw the bodies, and Law watched them dismount and examine the dead men.

Both men were strangers to Law, and he watched them closely. One was past middle age, and looked like a prosperous cattle rancher. He stood in the yard and looked around while his companion went into the bunkhouse and then the cook shack before going on to the house and disappearing inside.

Law went to his horse, mounted, and then rode into view and approached the yard. He rode towards the man, who stood watching him, a hand to his holstered pistol.

'Who are you?' Law demanded as he reined in. His keen gaze had already picked out the Double C brand on the flank of the horse.

'Charlie Cooper.' The man was tall and heavily built, with a fleshy face and a long nose set under a pair of suspicious blue eyes. 'Who are you?'

'Jed Law, State deputy marshal. You own Double C, I believe.'

'That's right. Are you watching this place?'

'I am. Where's your son Leroy?'

'Leroy? You don't think he had anything to do with this, do you?'

'Do you?' Law countered.

'No I don't. And I haven't seen Leroy in a couple of weeks. He doesn't live on Double C these days. Where are Ben and Julie Rutherford?'

'In town. Ben was beaten up

yesterday, but he's all right. You must have ridden by Big G on your way here. Did you see any activity there?'

'I didn't pass Big G. I took a short cut across the range. Have you any idea who did this shooting?'

'I know who did it. I was here yesterday when it happened. I killed those three hard cases.' He explained what had occurred, and Cooper shook his head.

'So it's started at last, huh?' he mused. 'I've been expecting it for a long time.'

'Do you believe Ben Rutherford rustled his neighbour's stock?' Law asked.

'Ben never struck me as a cow thief.'

Cooper's companion emerged from the house and paused on the porch. He was a thin man, wearing twin pistols in tied-down holsters on the crossed cartridge belts around his waist.

'Hey, Charlie, there's no sign of Rutherford or his daughter,' he called, and came off the porch hurriedly when he saw Law. 'Who are you?' he demanded brusquely as he came to them, his right hand on the butt of his gun. His pale blue eyes bored into Law, and he was poised for action.

'This is Pete Hubbard, my ranch foreman,' Cooper said. 'Pete, this is Jed Law, a deputy marshal. He was here yesterday when this shooting took place.'

'If you think Ben Rutherford is not a rustler, then why is he getting all this violence?' Law asked.

'Someone is out to take over the spread,' Hubbard said harshly, 'and I don't need two guesses at the man responsible.'

Law's keen gaze was watching his surroundings. He was expecting Tog Doughty to arrive with hard cases, and when he saw movement beyond the corral he pointed it out to Cooper.

'If you don't want to get caught up in another shooting then I suggest you both ride out now,' he said.

Cooper saw four riders coming around the corral.

'That's Tog Doughty with some of Geest's outfit,' he said. 'Perhaps you'd better ride out with us.'

Law smiled. 'I've been waiting for them to arrive,' he said. 'Get out of here.'

Cooper cursed, sprang into his saddle and started for the gate. Hubbard paused, his narrowed eyes on Law's set features.

'I'll stay if you want a hand against them,' he offered.

'I appreciate that.' Law shook his head. 'This is my job. You'd better go now.' Hubbard mounted and rode out. Law faced the oncoming riders, who rode into the yard by passing between the corral and the cook shack. They came in line, hands close to their guns, and Law recognized the foremost as Tog Doughty, who had been in the Big G ranch house with Seth Geest the evening before.

Doughty reined in. His eyes were narrowed under the brim of his black Stetson. He studied the five dead men lying in the dust before lifting his gaze to Law's motionless figure. Indecision showed momentarily on his hard features, and he was clearly puzzled by Law's presence.

'When did this happen?' he demanded.

'Yesterday. I killed those three after they shot the two Circle R men. I trailed the three back to Big G.' Law went on to explain how he had seen Doughty and Geest together, and heard what was said. 'So here I am,' he ended. 'I knew you were coming and I've been waiting for you to show up.'

'Are you a lawman? Did you arrest Geest last night and throw him in jail?'

'I am a deputy marshal from Amarillo, and I'm here to put a stop to the violence. You have orders from Seth Geest to occupy this place unlawfully and hold it against all-comers. I heard Geest tell you that. So if you're here to obey him then you've got a fight on your hands, Doughty.'

'Are you gonna face the four of us?' Doughty demanded. 'Where's your posse? You'll need at least a dozen men to stop us.'

'I killed Art Riley in town yesterday from an even break. I heard that Riley was the fastest gun around — until I showed up. So let us not waste any time. Put up or shut up.'

The hot breeze raised dust devils across the yard. Law stood motionless with his right hand down at his side, the protruding butt of his holstered pistol touching the inside of his wrist. His face was expressionless, his body coiled like a spring, and he waited for the first hostile movement on the part of the riders.

Doughty was uncomfortable with this confrontation. He preferred to have the edge any time he resorted to gun play, and he knew he was a lot slower on the draw than Art Riley had been. He had seen Riley in action several times, and if this lawman had beaten Riley from an even break then he had to be handled carefully. He shook his head, suddenly disconcerted. Whilst he was prepared to do anything to further Seth Geest's crooked plans, he was not ready to go up against the law.

'How'd I know you're a lawman?' he hedged.

Law lifted his left hand and tweaked aside his leather vest. Sunlight glinted on the shield-shaped law badge pinned to his shirt.

'Hell, I ain't getting mixed up with no law,' said one of the men siding Doughty. 'Leave me out of this.'

He wheeled his horse around and started back the way he had come, not looking back, and a second hard case followed him closely. Doughty stared after them, shaking his head.

'Yeller skunks!' he called, and then reached for his holstered pistol.

Law waited until Doughty had almost cleared leather before setting his right hand in motion. He drew his gun and fired in one swift, practised action, and Doughty reeled in his saddle as the thunderclap of the shot blasted through the silence. A lightning flash of pain stabbed through Doughty's chest and darkness fell before his eyes like a curtain as he tumbled from his saddle. He was not aware of hitting the ground.

The man who had remained with Doughty did not move. He shook his head when Law turned to him.

'I pass. I ain't sitting in on this game,' he said. 'Deal me out.'

'You're in whether you like it or not. You rode in with Doughty so you can stay. Get rid of your weapons.'

The hard case discarded his holstered pistol. His face was showing shock as he placed his hands on his saddle horn, and then, as if by an afterthought, he produced a hideout gun from his left armpit and tossed it into the dust. There was evident relief in his face as he sat motionless in his saddle.

'What's your name?' Law demanded.

'Sam Parfitt.'

'Where is Seth Geest right now?'

'At Big G. He was planning to take some men with him to town this morning; said he's got some cleaning up to do.'

'Who killed Dave Rutherford?'

'Don't ask me.' Parfitt shrugged. 'I don't know. He was shot in the back last week. No one knows who did it. He was alone on that little spread him and his two pards were running when it happened.'

'What two pards are they?'

'Leroy Cooper and Chance Geest.'

Law digested that information. He was watching his surroundings, and saw a furtive movement beyond the corral. He moved slightly to put Parfitt between himself and the movement, and had barely covered himself when a rifle shot cracked and echoed and Parfitt fell out of his saddle. Law was diving into cover before the hard case landed in the dust.

5

Law landed on his left shoulder in the thick dust of the yard, his deadly pistol ready in his hand. He heard the fading echoes of the shot and was prepared to fight, but silence returned and he realized that the gunman had pulled out. He got to his feet and checked Parfitt, who was dead, and then swung into his saddle. He sent the dun across the yard, around the corral, and spotted two riders heading away across the range in the direction of Big G.

It was clear to Law what his next move should be. Seth Geest had to be stopped. With the violence at an end, a thorough investigation into the situation could be carried out. Law pushed the dun into a gallop and began to gain on the two who had declined to fight in the Circle R yard, but he was still two hundred yards behind them when they reached Big G.

Law dismounted, left his horse in cover, and took his rifle when he edged forward into a position from which to observe Geest's headquarters. Several men were standing around in the yard, and there were six saddled horses tied to the hitching rail in front of the porch on the house. Using his field glasses, Law studied the men, noting that Geest was not in evidence.

The two riders he had followed went into the yard and were surrounded by the waiting men. When they had reported the incident in the Circle R yard, a man went into the house and, a few moments later, Seth Geest appeared on the porch.

Geest's reaction to the report on the latest shooting was immediate. He waved his arms excitedly as he gave orders, and the waiting men swung into their saddles and rode out of the yard. Law shook his head. He waited until the riders had passed him on their way to Circle R and then went back to his horse and began to circle the ranch. He wanted Geest.

He worked his way unseen around to the back of the house and left his horse in cover. A careful study of the area around the back of the ranch house satisfied him that there was not a guard on duty, and he drew his Colt as he stepped out from cover and moved steadily across to the back of the house. He made for the kitchen door and entered the house silently.

The cook was cleaning vegetables, and froze when he saw Law's big figure on the threshold. The gun in Law's hand was sufficient to cow him and he raised his hands.

'Take me to Geest,' Law said.

The cook shrugged and turned instantly to lead the way. They left the kitchen and went towards the front of the house.

'Seth, where are you?' the cook called.

'In my office,' Geest replied.

Law motioned with his gun and the cook entered the office. Law was a step behind, and pushed the cook aside to cover Geest, who was seated at his desk. Geest looked up, sighed, and sat very still.

'You again,' Geest observed.

'Did you expect me to go away?' Law motioned to the cook. 'Sit down in that corner and keep quiet.' He closed the door and confronted Geest. 'If you're armed then get rid of the hardware. You're under arrest again, and this time Crowley won't turn you loose. You can join him in his cell.'

'You got nothing on me.' Geest shook his head. 'I told you I haven't broken the law. I've been robbed blind, and only took steps to protect my ranch.'

'You sent Hap Jones into Circle R yesterday and two men were murdered. I witnessed that attack, and I'm holding you on a charge of murder. This morning Doughty showed up at Circle R with the intention of taking it over. He drew against me and I killed him. You're running rough-shod, Geest, and I'm putting you behind bars so I can carry out an investigation into the rustling and the murder of Dave Rutherford.'

'I know nothing about Rutherford's death,' Geest said doggedly. 'You won't get far before you're stopped. I've sent my outfit to nail you, and then I'll go through the county and take care of those who are stealing me blind.'

'You said Ben Rutherford was to blame,' Law observed. 'Are you saying now that others are involved in addition to Circle R?'

'I don't know who is behind it yet, but there's a big move to bust me, and I ain't standing still for it to happen.'

'What proof do you have that Rutherford is responsible for your losses?'

'My outfit caught two of the Circle R outfit on my range with a running iron, altering the brand on a lot of my stock. My cattle have been stolen and their tracks head on to Circle R range. That's proof enough for me. A man's got the right to protect his property, and that's what I've been doing.'

'You went off half-cocked, Geest, and I was sent in to investigate the trouble you're causing. I've had to kill a number of your outfit because they were riding rough-shod on your orders. You're responsible for all the violence and I'm taking you in and holding you until I can find out exactly what has been going on.'

'You won't get away with it,' Geest snarled.

'We'll see about that. Get up. We're leaving now, and if I get any trouble from your crew you'll be the first to stop lead.' Law motioned to the cook. 'Go out and prepare Geest's horse for travel. Bring it to the porch, and if any of the outfit are outside then warn them to stay out of it or Geest dies here and now.'

Geest got to his feet as the cook scuttled out of the office, and Law followed closely as the rancher walked to the front of the house.

'Hold it right there,' Law ordered as Geest prepared to open the door leading to the porch. 'We'll wait inside until the cook returns with your horse.'

'You don't expect him to come back, do you?' Geest chuckled as if he had heard a joke. 'They'll be waiting out there for you to show yourself, and when you do they'll fill you full of holes.'

'I'm holding all the aces in this play,' Law said sharply. 'If you want to see the jail in one piece then you'll warn off any of your crew who step out of line.'

'Not a chance! You got yourself into this corner and you'll have to get yourself out of it without my help.'

Law motioned for Geest to sit down on a chair that had its back to the wall beside the door while he stood at a window, peering out at the yard while keeping Geest under the menace of his gun. There was no movement outside, and silence pressed in around the yard, seemingly ominous and hostile.

Minutes dragged by, and Law was becoming impatient when he heard the sound of approaching hoofs in the yard.

He moved to the opposite side of the window and saw a dozen riders coming towards the ranch house.

'You're in trouble now!' exclaimed Geest. 'My outfit's coming back.'

'Does one of them wear a law star?' Law demanded. 'Unless I miss my guess, that's a posse coming in.'

Geest sprang up from his seat and peered through the window. He cursed and backed away from Law, his amusement changing to anger, and only the menace of Law's levelled pistol prevented him from attempting to get away. He glared at Law, his expression indicating that he was ready to resist.

'That's Sheriff Derry and a posse from Spanish Creek,' he rasped. 'What in hell is he doing here?'

'I sent him a message last night.' Law waggled his gun. 'Let's go out to the porch and greet him.'

Geest went outside with Law crowding him closely. The posse was coming across the yard towards the house, and Law noted several of Geest's men gathering by the corral.

The sheriff reined up in front of the porch, a middle-aged man, heavily overweight, whose sweating features were showing his discomfort in the saddle. He was holding a double-barrelled shotgun across his thighs, and the twin muzzles shifted slightly to cover Geest. The riders with him, several of whom were wearing law stars, spread out in a semicircle in front of the porch, and all were holding drawn weapons.

'So what's going on here?' Derry's blue eyes were narrowed against the glaring sunlight. His fleshy face was set in grim lines in which his thin mouth seemed like a rat trap. His eyes glared as if he were in a bad humour.

'I'm Jed Law, State deputy marshal. I've just arrested Seth Geest.'

'Then you've saved me a job. I had a report from Amarillo about you some time last week, telling me you were on your way and that I should help you all I can. I'm pleased to make your acquaintance. I'm here to see what all the shooting is about after I got the report you sent last night.' His gaze flickered to Geest. 'I have warned you about taking the law into your own hands, Geest, so what's set you off?'

'I've been protecting my property,' Geest replied. 'There's no law against that.'

'Let's get on to town and then we'll go over what's happened,' Derry said. He turned to his men. 'Joe, round up Geest's crew and we'll take 'em to town.'

One of the riders wearing a deputy badge motioned to several of the posse and they turned away to the corral. Law watched the remaining Big G outfit being disarmed and then ordered to get mounted. Geest remained sullenly quiet. Sheriff Derry stepped down from his saddle and towered over the rancher as he produced handcuffs.

'Hold 'em out,' he rasped. 'Don't give me any trouble, Seth, or it'll go bad for you. I wanta do this the easy way.'

'We'd better call in at Circle R on the

way to town,' Law said. 'The rest of Geest's gunnies might be there.'

Within minutes the cavalcade was heading for Buffalo Creek, the posse riding ahead with the prisoners. Law, accompanied by the sheriff, rode at the rear of the party, and took the opportunity to bring Derry up to date with the incidents that had occurred. The sheriff shook his head when he learned of Crowley's arrest.

'What in hell came over him?' he mused. 'He was a good lawman in Spanish Creek, and I thought he was doing a fair job around here. It looks like Geest got to him, huh? I'm gonna put Joe Harmon into the office in town. Joe is a good man, and won't stand for any bad doings. No one will be able to sway him from his duty. Hey, Joe, drop back here and meet your new boss. We'll all take orders from him while he's operating in this county.'

Harmon was a big man in his saddle, broad-shouldered and capable-looking. His dark eyes sparkled as he grinned at

Law and stuck out a big hand.

'Glad to make your acquaintance,' he said as they shook hands. 'I'm looking forward to taking over in Buffalo Creek.'

When they neared Circle R, Derry sent Harmon ahead with the posse while he sat his horse with his shotgun pointing at Geest. Law rode with the posse and they loped into the Rutherford yard, where a number of Geest's men were standing around. Law noted that the dead men had been placed in a grim line in front of the bunkhouse. With several law stars showing among the posse, the hard cases were disinclined to resist and were disarmed. Derry rode up with Geest, and the posse continued to town.

Law heaved a silent sigh of relief when they reached Buffalo Creek. A crowd gathered as Geest's outfit was ushered into the law office. The prisoners were crowded into the cells and locked in. Derry confronted Crowley, but the ex-deputy had nothing to say to his former boss.

A great weight seemed to have been removed from Law's shoulders. Since his arrival he had not had time to think about anything except defending himself against the hard cases Geest had sent against him. Now his mind was freed of tension and he sat down at the desk in the office and read through the reports Crowley had made, hoping to get a slant on what had been going on. It did not take him long to discover that the ex-deputy had not kept an accurate record of the events that had taken place.

Sheriff Derry was sitting across the desk from Law, content to let Law handle the investigation.

'There's a lot going on under cover around here,' Law said. 'I overheard Geest say that he had partners.'

Derry nodded. 'It looks that way to me. From what I've seen of Crowley's reports, I guess he hasn't told me half of what's happened.'

'I need to find out who killed Dave Rutherford, and why,' Law mused. 'Are you sticking around town for a spell, Sheriff?'

'Not me.' Derry shook his head. 'I'm gonna leave Jack Dawling with Joe Harmon. They're both experienced deputies, and with the townsmen they can call on as possemen I reckon you'll lick this trouble in no time.'

'Good. I'll look up Ben Rutherford and his daughter and get some background on what happened to Dave. Thanks for turning up when you did, Sheriff. I might have had big trouble hauling Geest away from his outfit.'

'If there's anything I can do to help then just let me know.' Derry nodded. 'I reckon you should keep the guilty hard cases in jail to face trial, and send the rest of Geest's outfit packing, with orders not to come back to the county on pain of arrest. There are too many gun hands around here, and until they fade away there ain't much hope of bringing peace back to the county.'

Law nodded and left the office. He

looked around the wide main street as if seeing it for the first time, and set off along the sidewalk to the hotel, pushing through the thronging townsfolk on the sidewalk. He saw Julie Rutherford standing in front of the hotel and went to her, his keen gaze noting how sad she looked, which was not surprising considering that she had buried her brother the day before. He frowned when he noted that she was wearing a gunbelt, the holster of which contained a .38 Colt.

'I don't believe what I saw,' she said in greeting. 'You've got most of the Big G crew, including Seth Geest, but where is Chance Geest? He should have been one of the first you arrested.'

'I didn't see him around. I'll pick him up as soon as I can get to him. I need to talk to you, Julie. I'm about to get a meal, so would you accompany me? We can talk while I eat.'

'The hotel has a dining-room. I was fixing to eat. What do you want to talk to me about?'

'Your brother's murder. I was hoping you'd stop wearing that gun now I'm in action around here.'

She shook her head and grimaced, but did not reply, and drew the .38 as they entered the hotel. Law heard the rasp of the weapon and glanced sideways at her, saw that she was holding out the weapon to him and took it, stuffing it into his waistband near his spine as they sat down at a corner table in the small dining-room. Law positioned himself with his back to a wall and, when Julie tried to sit opposite, he asked her to sit on his left, wanting a clear view of the entrance. He sensed that she was bubbling with aggression, even more so than she had been the night before, and guessed that frustration was gnawing at her.

'How is your father?' he enquired.

'Not right by a long rope.' She shook her head. 'Doc Rouse looked at him when I got back to town last night, and he thinks the beating Pa took has affected his brain in some way. I don't know which way to turn right now. Pa has always been there to make the decisions and do what is necessary. Now I'm in the big saddle, and I don't have an outfit, our stock has been rustled, and I have no idea how to handle the situation.'

'Circle R has lost stock?' Law frowned. 'I thought the boot was on the other foot. Seth Geest has accused you of rustling Big G cattle, and you reckon you're the victims.'

'You've only got to ride across our range to see that we've been robbed blind,' she said bitterly. 'And then go take a look at Big G and count their cows. I think Geest has robbed us, and branded us as rustlers to cover up what he's done. Anyone who really knows my father is aware that he wouldn't steal a single cow.'

A waitress came to the table and they ordered a meal. Law drew his pistol and placed it on the table close to his right hand as the waitress departed.

'So what happened to your brother?' Law prompted.

'He went into the ranching business with Chance Geest and Leroy Cooper last year. They took over the old McCarthy place, west of Big G, and called it DCL. I told Dave it was a wrong move, trying to work with Chance Geest, because he's a waster, and Leroy isn't much better, but Dave wouldn't listen to me and went ahead anyway, and after all their big talk they had to make out with a ten-cow operation and a lot of luck. None of them could lay their hands on the money they needed to finance their business, I could see they were heading for disaster before they even started ranching, and when they failed to keep up the payments on their mortgage, the bank foreclosed. Dave was out there last week, picking up his gear, when he was shot in the back.'

'Who found him?' Law asked.

'Grat Kibbee, the banker. He and Parker Strutt rode out there to check over the spread after it had been vacated, and they found Dave lying dead in the yard.'

Law got a mental picture of Strutt — the diminutive attorney-at-law with the shifty gaze — when the girl mentioned him, and grimaced as he considered. In his experience as a lawman, he fancied that Strutt was guilty about something, and made a mental note to talk to the lawyer as soon as possible.

'Did the coroner examine Dave's body?' he asked.

'Yes. It was Doc Rouse. He said Dave had been killed by a .41 slug, probably fired from a derringer, or some such weapon. He had been shot in the back at very close range, and had been dead at least two days when his body was found.'

'What day was he killed?'

'Last Monday.'

'Have you any idea of his movements over his last two days?'

'None at all.' She spoke in a whisper,

her voice at breaking point. 'We weren't talking much then.'

'And Crowley investigated the murder, I guess,' Law mused. 'I'll have to talk to people. I've been forced to defend myself against Geest's hard cases since my arrival, but I should be able to get down to brass tacks after this. Ah, here's the food, and I'll bet it tastes as good as it smells.'

He straightened in his seat as the waitress approached with plates of food, and silence ensued while they ate. Law ate steadily, as if he sensed that it could be his last meal, but Julie merely picked at her plate, and had barely eaten anything by the time Law had finished.

Law's thoughts were busy while he ate, and he realized that he needed to start his investigation from the beginning. He had been side-tracked by the violence that had beset him on his arrival, but now Geest was in jail and his hard case crew disarmed, he should have the opportunity to handle the case properly. Lost in his thoughts, he struggled against impatience as he considered where to start his probing.

'I'd like to go back to Circle R now Geest and his bunch are out of circulation,' Julie said when she finally pushed her plate aside. 'I have so much to do. I could leave Pa here in town with Doc Rouse to care for him, and by the time Pa is feeling better I'd have the spread up and running again.'

'I would advise you to hang fire for a few days,' Law said. 'Nothing is certain yet, and there could be a lot more trouble to come before the situation improves. Why was Dave murdered? Was it during an argument over the business he was involved in? Chance Geest and Leroy Cooper weren't the ideal business partners. I shall be talking to them shortly, and until I get my investigation on the move I'd like you to stick around town where you'll be a lot safer than on your ranch.'

She sighed and shook her head, and Law could tell that she would probably ignore his advice.

'Is there anything you can tell me about the trouble that is not hearsay or imagination?' he asked. 'I deal in facts, and if you know anything that can be proved then tell me about it and you'll save me valuable time. I want to know about any wrong-doing, no matter who was involved.'

'Dave told me he wished he hadn't gone into business with Chance and Leroy. He didn't say anything more than that, but I'm sure those two know a lot about what was going on. Grat Kibbee was reluctant to lend them money because he felt that they were not to be trusted, and then the overland stage was robbed. Dave hinted some about that, and I got the impression he thought Chance and Leroy did it. Seth Geest had to stand as guarantor before they got their mortgage.'

Law reached out to pick up his pistol, but a shadow fell across him and he looked up quickly. A man had entered the dining-room by the side door just along to Law's right and he recognized Hawk Bassell. The Big G gun man was holding a pistol in his right hand with the muzzle pointing at Law's head.

'Try and beat me now,' Bassell said roughly. 'Go on, make a play for your gun and see how far you can get before I kill you!'

6

Law looked into the black eye of the steady muzzle gaping at him from the distance of six inches and froze. Bassell waggled the gun. His face was taut but his lips were twisted into a travesty of a smile, his eyes glittering balefully. He looked like a man who had passed the point of no return.

'Come on,' he urged. 'Show me how fast you are now. Your gun is on the table. Pick it up and try to use it.'

'You're in a lot of trouble without this,' Law said quietly. 'Put up your gun before you make matters worse. We don't want gun play in here. Innocent folks could get hurt. Let's go outside. You wouldn't want to shoot me in front of witnesses, would you?'

'You made a fool of me with your fast draw,' Bassell said harshly. 'I ain't ever gonna live that down. I'm finished as a gun hand. I stood by and did nothing while you beat Riley to the draw. That ain't good in my business and I'm gonna kill you. Get up and leave by the alley door.'

Law stood up slowly, leaving his pistol on the table. He was aware of Julie's .38 nestling in his waistband, and eased sideways around Bassell as he moved towards the alley door. Bassell backed off, staying out of arm's length, and Law stepped out into the alley, spinning around to face Bassell as the gun man moved into the doorway.

Despite having to use Julie's gun in the back of his waistband, Law made a fast draw and cocked the weapon as it came to hand. Bassell saw the movement but his reaction was slow. Shock stained his face as he realized that Law had a second gun. He squeezed his trigger, and, as the shot boomed out, Law dropped to one knee.

Bassell's shot plucked at the brim of Law's hat, sending it whirling from his head. Before the gunman could fire again Law triggered the .38, sending two bullets into Bassett's chest. The gunman was flung backwards an unsteady step by the deadly impact of the bullets. An agonized cry escaped his taut lips as he fell to the floor and his gun fired a second shot as he went down. Law heard the bullet whine past his left ear and thud into the building across the alley.

The harsh echoes of the shooting fled across the town as Law regained his feet and turned to pick up his hat. He was breathing heavily, his face grim. A sigh escaped him as he looked down at Bassell, and he shook his head as he considered the futility of what was happening. Too many men were dying at the altar of greed and selfishness, and the man or men responsible were as yet unknown.

Julie came to Law's side. Her face was pale, her bottom lip nipped between her teeth, and there was an unholy light in her pale eyes.

'Is it always like this for you?' she demanded.

'That's the nature of my job,' he replied, moving to the table and picking up his pistol. He slid the weapon into its holster. 'Someone has to do it, and I've grown accustomed to working for the law.'

Joe Harmon appeared in the alley doorway, gun in hand and law star glinting on his shirt front. He was breathing heavily, as if he had run all the way from the law office. Relief showed on his fleshy face when he saw Law apparently unhurt.

'You had me worried for a spell,' he said, peering down at Bassell. 'Do you know who he is?'

Law explained, and Harmon nodded.

'It was on the cards he would come for you, beating him as you did. He couldn't accept the fact that you are faster. I'll have his body removed.'

'I shall be leaving town shortly,' Law said. 'I want to get some background on Dave Rutherford's murder. There are a couple of men in town I need to talk to before I visit the scene of the murder.

Maybe I can have a posse man to accompany me when I ride out. It would help having someone along who knows the range. I expect to be out of town a couple of days.'

'I'll ride with you,' Julie said instantly. 'I need something to do that will occupy my mind.'

'I'll think about that,' Law promised. 'See you later.'

He left the hotel and walked to the bank. Heat shimmered along the street and he felt sweat breaking out on his face. As he reached the door of the bank it was jerked open from the inside and Parker Strutt appeared. The lawyer paused when he recognized Law, and then moved forward quickly to depart but Law blocked him in the doorway, forcing him to stop.

'I need to talk to you, Strutt. Where's your office? I'll visit you there after I've talked to Kibbee.'

'What do you want to talk to me about?' Strutt stumbled over his words, his uneasiness plain to Law's practised gaze.

'I'll get around to that when I see you.'

'I'll be in my office next to the general store.' Strutt pushed by Law and almost ran along the sidewalk.

Law entered the bank and was shown into Kibbee's office. The banker was seated behind a big leather-topped desk, and arose quickly to advance with an outstretched hand.

'How can I help you, Marshal?' he asked. 'I heard the shooting a few minutes ago. You're still busy bringing law and order back to the community, huh?'

'I'll get there in the end,' Law responded. 'You found Dave Rutherford's body last week. Tell me about it.'

'There's nothing to tell. Dave was stretched out on his face in the yard of DCL with a bullet between his shoulder blades. I was with Parker Strutt at the time, and sent him back to town for Doc Rouse, who said Dave had been killed about two days before we found him. There was nothing to point to what had happened. I would have thought he'd been shot from long distance, but Doc dug a .41 slug out of him, and I never heard of a rifle using that calibre.'

'Julie told me Dave had been shot in the back at very close quarters, probably by someone using a derringer. What were you doing out on the range?'

'I needed to check over the spread. I had to foreclose on Dave and his friends because they had failed at ranching, and I stepped in to help them cut their losses. They'd bought a small herd, and it was stolen within a month. It was a rotten business. The partners blamed one another for their losses, and bad blood resulted. Dave and Chance Geest fell out, and fought in the street here in town over their differences.'

Law nodded attentively. 'How long after that fight was Dave murdered?' he asked.

'Just a couple of weeks. The ranch

was done for by then. That's all I can tell you. When we rode out to inspect the spread, there was Dave, stretched out dead in the yard.'

'Thanks.' Law departed, and stood on the sidewalk outside the bank while he considered, his keen gaze missing nothing of his surroundings. He saw Strutt standing on the sidewalk a block away, and went towards the diminutive lawyer, who retreated into his office as Law neared him.

Strutt was seated at his desk when Law walked into the office. He was plainly uneasy, nervous, his prominent Adam's apple moving up and down as he gulped at an apparent lump in his throat. He sat back in his chair and gazed at Law with the intensity of a rabbit looking at a stoat that was preparing to kill him.

'What did Kibbee tell you?' he demanded, leaning forward and making a big show of straightening papers on his desk.

'What are you worried about?' Law

countered. 'I've been law dealing for seven years, and seen a lot of guilty men in that time. Some couldn't conceal their guilt, and it's plain to me that you're one of that type, Strutt. You've got something bad on your mind and I'd like to know what it is.'

'You must be joking!' Strutt's Adam's apple bobbed nervously. 'I'm a law abiding man, and I don't have the time or the inclination to listen to that kind of talk. What is it you want to see me about?'

'Why did you ride out to the DCL spread with Kibbee on the afternoon you found Dave Rutherford dead?'

'I often go with Kibbee. It's the only chance I get to ride out of town for a change of scenery. Do you suspect me of killing Rutherford?'

'I don't suspect anyone.' Law's eyes were narrowed, and seemed to bore into the lawyer. 'Who do you think shot Dave in the back?'

'What does it matter what I think? That won't help your investigation.

You're wasting my time, Marshal.' Strutt gulped and broke off suddenly and produced a handkerchief to wipe his brow. 'You think I'm guilty of something, huh? Well the fact is, I'm not a well man. I have a health problem, and that's why I'm looking ill at ease.'

'Sure, if you say so. Have you consulted Doc Rouse?'

'More than once, but he cannot help me. Is there anything else you want?'

'Not right now. But I'll come back to you if I think of anything.'

'Feel free to call any time.' Strutt looked immensely relieved, and got to his feet as Law turned to depart.

'When I call again I shall want to know what is bothering you,' Law said, taking a final glance at Strutt before leaving. 'You sure got the look of a guilty man, Strutt.'

He departed with Strutt's effusive protests ringing in his ears and went along the street to the law office, wondering about Strutt's attitude. He decided that the only way he might make progress with the lawyer was by waging a war of nerves on the man.

A great number of townsfolk were on the street, congregated around the law office, and Law went forward, but turned aside when he reached the doctor's office. He entered to find Doc Rouse seated at his desk.

'Howdy, Marshal, how can I help you?' Rouse demanded.

'I'm investigating Dave Rutherford's murder. What can you tell me about it?'

'Not a lot. Parker Strutt came for me last week declaring Dave was lying dead in the yard of his spread. I went out to DCL and found Grat Kibbee there. Dave Rutherford was stretched out in the dust. I examined him and decided he'd been dead at least two days, and when I got the body back to town and carried out a post-mortem I found the bullet that killed him was a .41, which doesn't tell us a lot because there must be at least fifty .41 guns around town. It's not a lot to go on, and I cannot speculate on who might have killed Dave.'

'Do you know if he had any enemies?'

Rouse shook his head. 'I hesitate to make a guess. He was in a lot of trouble over the business he had gone into. His two partners were not happy with the way things had turned out, and they blamed Dave for the trouble.'

'Why would they do that?'

'It would be better if you asked Chance and Leroy about it.'

Law smiled. 'I intend to, the instant I pick them up.' He nodded. 'Thanks Doc. How is Ben Rutherford today?'

'He's not too well.'

'It's a big coincidence that Dave was murdered, and this week his father was attacked and badly beaten.'

'It's a bad business.' Rouse nodded. 'You do have witnesses to Ben Rutherford's beating, so you know where to look for the culprits.'

'I've just talked to Parker Strutt, and he tells me he's been suffering ill health. What's wrong with him?'

'I haven't seen Strutt professionally in years.' Rouse shook his head. 'If he's been ill then I know nothing about it.'

Law nodded and departed. So Strutt had lied to him about his health so there had to be another reason for his uneasiness. He filed the information in his mind and went along to the law office, having to push through the crowd to enter. Sheriff Derry, on the point of departing, was instructing Harmon on how to carry out his duties.

'The first thing to do is disperse that crowd outside,' Law said.

'I'll do that,' Derry said. 'I'm heading back to Spanish Creek now. Keep me informed of what happens around here, Joe, and if there's anything you need from me then send a message.'

'You don't need to worry, Sheriff,' Harmon replied. 'We'll do it right.'

'One thing before you go, Sheriff,' Law said. 'I was told at headquarters that if there is rustling on this range then I could be certain that Butch Rainey has a finger in it. He handles most of the rustling north of the border and is probably in cahoots with Pancho Vasquez, who operates in Mexico.'

'I know of all the bad men in these parts,' Derry replied. 'I've chased Rainey and his crooked bunch to the border more than once and lost them. I don't think Rainey is involved in this particular business. It hasn't got his earmarks. I'd be surprised if he is mixed up in it.'

Law nodded and the sheriff departed. Law picked up the cell keys and tossed them to Harmon.

'I want to question Crowley,' he said. 'Bring him out, Joe. I expect it will be a waste of time but I've got to talk to him.'

Harmon fetched the ex-deputy, and Law sat behind the desk and gazed at Crowley, who sat motionless and sullen on the chair before the desk, his attitude proclaiming his intention to remain remote.

'I'm investigating the murder of Dave Rutherford,' Law said. 'Tell me about it.'

'There was no evidence pointing to the killer.' Crowley shrugged. 'That's all I learned. I spoke with Chance Geest and Leroy Cooper and they said they were away on a trip when Dave was killed.'

'Did you check on their movements at the time of Dave's death?' Law leaned forward and placed his elbows on the desk, his gaze holding Crowley's gaze.

'They gave me names of men they had seen over Hamilton way but I didn't get around to checking their stories. That's all I can tell you.'

Law asked more questions, trying to get Crowley to add to the bare facts, but nothing more emerged and Harmon returned the ex-deputy to his cell, leaving Law gazing after Crowley and wondering about his description. The scar on Crowley's cheek seemed to have a special significance and he was certain he knew why, but at the moment the answer eluded him.

'I'm gonna have to start from scratch

with this investigation,' Law told Harmon when the deputy rejoined him. 'A week has passed since the murder, but it's not too late to gather evidence. Give me a man who knows the area and I'll ride out.'

'Jack Dawling can ride with you. He's along at the store right now, buying in ammunition. I'm not taking any chances with this situation. I don't know what's going on yet and, with a jail full of prisoners, it could blow up in our faces. I'll keep an eye open around town for any of Rainey's bunch. I've been up against them several times, and in Spanish Creek we have some dodgers on them. If Rainey is operating around here then I'll get to know it.'

'I would appreciate your efforts.' Law nodded. 'You'll need to get charges made out for your prisoners. I'll attend to my side of it when I get back. Seth Geest is guilty of arranging murder and I'll put the details in my report. You can release those hard cases we haven't got evidence against. Warn them off and make sure they don't return to town.'

'I'll get to work digging for facts,' Harmon promised.

'I must visit the store before riding out.' Law was feeling an urge to get more deeply involved in his job, aware that with Seth Geest in jail the number of gunnies wanting to face him should lessen considerably. He left the office.

Outside the crowd was dispersing and the sheriff was already in his saddle. Law went along the sidewalk, and met Jack Dawling emerging from the store with a bulging gunny sack in his left hand.

'Jack, I've arranged with Joe for you to accompany me,' Law said. 'I'm riding out shortly to get to grips with Dave Rutherford's murder. It's a bit of a cold trail now, and I have to start at the beginning, but it's got to be done. Can you be ready to ride in fifteen minutes?'

'Sure. Our horses are outside the law office. I'll see you there.' Dawling nodded and went on his way.

Law went into the store, and was confronted immediately by Julie Rutherford. Her face was pale but composed as she regarded him.

'I heard what you said to the deputy,' she said firmly. 'Does that mean you won't let me ride with you? I offered to show you around, and it was my brother that was murdered. I have a personal stake in finding the killer.'

'I'm sorry, but I can't let you ride with me, Julie.' Law shook his head emphatically when she began to protest. 'It's too dangerous for a woman to go along. I wouldn't be able to concentrate on my job if I had you to worry over. Your place is to stay with your father and do what you can to help him, and if you think about it you'll know I'm right.'

She nodded, her expression harsh, and left him standing, hurrying from the store. Law sighed and went to the counter. He bought .45 cartridges for his pistol and 44.40 shells for his rifle, and provisions for several days. When he went back outside he was pleased to see that the crowd had dispersed and the sheriff had departed with his posse. The town looked normal now, and Law's spurs jingled as he went back to the office.

He put his supplies on the dun and entered the office. Dawling was waiting for him. Harmon was emerging from the cell block, the cell keys in his hand.

'Before you leave,' Harmon said. 'Seth Geest wants a word with you. Says he's got something on his mind.'

'I'll see him now.'

Law went into the cell block and confronted Geest, who was standing at the door of his cell, grasping the bars as if he would tear them loose.

'What do you want?' Law demanded. 'I've got a lot to do and you've been wasting my time ever since I arrived in town.'

'Are you going after my boy for

Rutherford's murder?' Geest rapped.

'Chance is high on my list of suspects.' Law nodded. 'He and Leroy Cooper were in business with Dave, and I heard there was trouble between them. Have you any idea where Chance might be? You said he's not living at the ranch, and he hasn't got DCL now. So where is he?'

'I don't know. He never tells me anything these days, but I heard he's staying with a woman in the hills west of town.'

Law gazed at Geest, wondering if there was a thaw coming in the rancher's attitude.

'Do you want to talk about what's been going on around the range?' he asked.

'I told you about the rustling. Rutherford damn nigh cleared my range of stock.'

'Can you prove Circle R was responsible?'

'I tracked two hundred head of my beef to a cattle buyer on the border. He showed me a bill of sale signed by Ben Rutherford.'

'Why didn't you take the matter to the local law instead of trying to settle it yourself? Men have been killed, and it could all have been avoided if you'd gone about it in the right way.'

Geest chuckled harshly. 'The only way a man can get anything done around here is to do it himself. You saw the specimen of law dealer we had in the shape of Scar Crowley.'

'I'll check on your story when I get back. You'll stay in jail until I have worked out what happened. Make a full statement to Joe Harmon and we'll take it from there.'

Geest shrugged and Law turned to the office to see Joe Harmon standing in the doorway. The deputy had been listening.

'I'll get a statement from him,' Harmon said. 'I reckon the feel of the bars around him are playing on his mind.'

Law nodded and took his leave. He found Jack Dawling outside, waiting for him, and they mounted and rode out. Law's relief increased as they hit the open trail.

'We're going to DCL,' Law said. 'Do you know where that is, Jack?'

'Sure thing. It's the old McCarthy place. I didn't think those three youngsters would make a go of ranching when I heard about their venture. I reckoned Dave Rutherford was asking for trouble, throwing in with a couple of hard cases like Chance Geest and Leroy Cooper. Those two never did a day's work in their lives, and they left all the work at DCL to Dave. I'm not surprised there was trouble between them.'

They travelled across undulating range. Law cast an eye at the western horizon, gauging that they had about five hours of daylight left. He planned to check out the place where Dave Rutherford had been killed, spend the night at the DCL, and set out early in the morning, hopefully following tracks left by Dave's killer.

'We're being followed,' Dawling announced about an hour later.

'I got the same feeling,' Law replied. 'We better check it out.'

They crossed a skyline and reined in below it, leaving their mounts in cover and easing back to the crest. A sigh escaped Law when he saw a lone figure coming towards them and recognized Julie Rutherford.

'That girl sure doesn't take no for an answer,' he said. 'I was hoping she'd stay out of it now. Come on, let's ride fast. Perhaps we can shake her off.'

They returned to their horses and rode on at a gallop, hammering across the rough ground. Dawling took the lead, and an hour later he reined up on a crest and motioned towards a small ranch nestling between two low hills. The house was hardly more than a cabin, and there was a small corral off to the left.

'There's DCL,' Dawling remarked. 'It looks kind of quiet, huh? No stock around and no horses. And Dave

Rutherford lay dead in the yard for two days before he was found.'

They rode in steadily, and Law watched his surroundings as they neared the spread. They entered the yard and he dismounted, motioning for Dawling to keep away from the centre. He walked around carefully, looking at the tracks that were present in the thick dust. Most of the prints were days old, and he memorized some of them.

Law had worked his way close to the house by the time Julie Rutherford appeared at the gate, and he motioned to her to keep away from the centre of the yard. She dismounted beside Dawling.

'I saw some riders off to my right as I came over that skyline back there,' she said excitedly. 'Six men circling around this place. They looked like they were on the prod. I think you'd better get ready for trouble, just in case.'

The ranch was silent and still. The sun was already well on its course for the distant horizon. Law looked around and saw a movement off behind the corral, and when he looked in the opposite direction he spotted a pair of riders closing in.

'Don't hurry it, but get inside the cabin,' he said quietly. 'Take your weapons with you, Jack. Those riders will be on us in a few minutes.'

'I've seen them,' Dawling replied. 'We won't have to look too hard for evidence, huh? They're coming in to hand it to us on a plate.'

Julie trailed her reins, snatched a rifle out of her saddle boot, and went into the cabin, followed immediately by Dawling. Law turned slowly, his keen gaze raking his surroundings, and when he caught sight of sunlight glinting on metal in the brush off to his left he drew his rifle from its scabbard, took two boxes of ammunition from a saddle-bag, and ran towards the cabin.

He was still three paces from the door when a volley of rifle shots crackled and slugs hammered into the front wall of the cabin. He threw away caution and lunged for cover, hurling himself through the open doorway and rolling on the earth floor inside with slugs striking around him and dust flying as the shooting intensified.

7

Law levered a cartridge into the breech of his Winchester as he pushed himself up from the floor. He lunged to a window and crashed the muzzle of the rifle through the glass. Two men were riding in fast across the yard from the right, tossing lead haphazardly at the cabin. He glanced around and saw two more riders coming in from the left, and ducked as a bullet splintered through the wall and whined across the cabin.

Glancing around, Law noted that Dawling was at the rear window, already firing his Winchester. Julie was down on the ground, rifle forgotten, her body pressed flat. Her face was turned towards him and her eyes were closed.

A pane of glass above his head shattered into jagged shards that rained down on his Stetson. The shooting increased until it blotted out all else, a rolling, hammering concerto of blustering pistol talk that raked at the nerves. Bullet holes appeared as if by magic in the front wall of the cabin as splinters flew from the riddled woodwork. A shot tugged at Law's hat and he ducked. A frying-pan hanging on the back wall clanged and then jumped off its hook. Dawling uttered a cry that was almost lost in the tumult and fell on his face, writhing in pain.

Law braved the storm of fire and pushed himself upright, thrusting the muzzle of his rifle through the broken window. He aimed to his right and triggered the weapon, sending a stream of deadly 44.40 slugs at the attackers. He could see the two riders in that direction, now dismounted and coming forward almost shoulder to shoulder, and ignored the slugs that were coming from his left and slanting through the front wall in their blind flight. His first shot took one of the men through the right arm above the elbow and the second slammed into his chest. He switched his aim and sent two slugs into the body of the second man.

The pair went down in a tangle of threshing limbs, and Law noted an immediate slackening of hostile fire. He moved across the window and peered to his left, his deadly rifle steady as he looked for targets, and was just in time to see two attackers running back out of his line of fire, angling for the corner of the cabin.

Turning to a side window, Law saw that Julie was crawling across the floor to go to Dawling's aid. The deputy was inert now, face upwards and arms outflung. Law could see blood staining the front of Dawling's shirt, low in the right shoulder.

The two men who had run to the side of the cabin to avoid Law's deadly fire out front were crouching against the side wall. The shooting had dwindled somewhat, and Law caught the sound of their voices outside. He judged the position of the sound and sent three quick shots through the wall of the cabin. As the sound of the shooting fled he heard a voice crying out in agony, and fired again.

Glass tinkled from a back window and Law spun to face the danger. A bearded face appeared at the window and Law fired without seeming to take aim. There was a cry and the face vanished, to be replaced instantly by a hand holding a pistol, which fired randomly into the cabin. Law aimed for the hand and fired, shattering flesh and bone. The pistol fell inside the cabin as the hand was rapidly withdrawn.

Law estimated that at least four of the six assailants were out of action. The shooting had ceased momentarily and he reloaded his pistol as the echoes grumbled away into the distance. He dropped to one knee beside the prostrate form of Jack Dawling and saw at a glance that the deputy was dead. He got to his feet, leaned his rifle against the wall beside the door, and then went outside, his pistol cocked.

Two attackers were lying inertly off to the right. Law studied them for a moment and then moved to the corner on his left. He peered around the corner and saw an assailant stretched out on his back with two splotches of blood on his shirt front. The man was moving slightly, and Law kicked his discarded gun away and walked on to the rear corner. He found the man with the bearded face lying dead on his back by the rear window.

Law went on quickly, and heard the sound of departing hoofs as he neared the opposite rear corner. He lifted his Colt when he saw the two surviving riders moving away rapidly, and fired instantly. The nearest rider jerked under the impact of questing lead and swayed sideways, almost falling out of his saddle. Law tried to get a shot at the second rider, who was mounted on a powerful black stallion that had a lot of white showing on its right rear leg. The next instant both riders had galloped into dead ground and were no longer visible.

He went right around the cabin before entering it again. Julie was still hunkered over the body of Jack Dawling. Law holstered his gun and grasped the girl by the shoulders, lifting her upright. Her face was pale. She looked badly shocked. Law shook her gently.

'Come on, snap out of it,' he said softly. 'Jack is dead. We can't help him. I want you to look at the men outside. See if you can recognize any of them. Three are dead; the fourth is barely alive. Let's go look at them. You want to know who killed Dave, don't you?'

Her brother's name put some steel into Julie's mind and she straightened, her eyes narrowing. Law heard her sigh, and then she walked out of the cabin. He led her around to the side where the wounded attacker was lying and she gazed at the man's face for long moments before shaking her head.

'No,' she said finally. 'I've never seen him before.'

'That's OK.'

Law led her around to the back of the cabin, and they both gazed down at the dead attacker. Julie shook her head.

'He's a stranger,' she said.

They went around to the front of the cabin where the two men who had attacked Law from the right were lying almost side by side. Julie shook her head and turned away.

Law was already checking their surroundings. Nothing moved out there now and he turned in a full circle, his keen eyes looking for movement. He was satisfied that the surviving attackers had pulled out and realized that he had much to do. He needed to follow the two escaping men to see where they were going, and to check their incoming tracks to find out where they had come from.

'Will you be OK to ride back to town on your own?' he asked.

'What are you going to do?' she countered. 'I'd rather stick with you.'

'Haven't you had enough yet? You've

been lucky so far, so you're going back to town whether you like it or not. I've got work to do and I'll have to move fast. You go back to town and tell Joe Harmon, the new deputy, what happened here. Get the Doc out to look at that wounded man, although I expect he'll die before he can get treatment. Will you do that?'

Julie was trembling in shock and her eyes proclaimed her inner state of confusion, but she nodded. Law led her to where their horses were standing with trailing reins and pushed her into her saddle. She looked at him dully, barely recording her surroundings. He put the reins into her hands and then stepped back and slapped the rump of the horse. The animal took off fast and she swayed in her saddle but kept going. He watched her until she rode out of sight along the trail to town, and a sigh of relief escaped him as he brought his mind back to what he had to do.

He fetched his Winchester from

inside the cabin and slid it into his saddle scabbard. Mounting the dun, he swung the animal quickly to ride around the cabin. His gaze picked up the tracks of the two men who had ridden away and he touched spurs to the dun's flanks, pushing the animal into a run. This was where his work really began. At last he had a definite lead to the bad men, and he meant to take full advantage of it.

He rode away from the cabin at a fast clip, ready for any eventuality. Tracks were plain on the ground and he followed them. He was wondering about the six strangers who had attacked them. If they were not local riders then where had they come from, and who were they working for? So far, all his trouble had come from Seth Geest's outfit, and he had shot them full of holes. Now, it seemed, another outfit was taking a hand.

He had covered barely two miles from the cabin when he spotted a man sprawled on the ground; a horse grazing nearby. He approached cautiously, saw the man was dead, and gazed at the still figure for some moments, comparing the inert features with the descriptions of the many wanted dodgers he could remember, but nothing stirred his memory and he dismounted and bent over the man. A search of the body revealed no clues to his identity, and the saddle-bags contained nothing personal. Law turned away, picked up the line of prints left by the surviving rider, and studied them until he would know them anywhere. He rode on, following the tracks.

Two hours passed. Law had been expecting the trail to lead him anywhere but Buffalo Creek, but daylight was almost gone when he saw the town in the distance, and the tracks were heading straight into the main street. He realized that he had made a half circle on the ride back to town, and expected Julie to have arrived long before him. He did not want to see her again yet, and decided to give the law office a miss.

Shadows were creeping into corners and yellow lamp light flared at many windows along the street as he rode by the law office and followed the tracks to the livery barn. He had a picture of the black horse in his mind as he dismounted wearily at the door of the stable and led his horse inside. An ostler was lighting a lantern just inside the doorway, but the shadows inside the building were dense.

'Just the man I want to see,' Law said. He described the horse he had been following. 'Has it come in here in the last half hour?'

'I'm Tom Smith. Yeah, I've seen it. I was forking hay into the loft when the rider of that horse showed up, mebbe half an hour ago. Is he a friend of your'n?'

'I'd sure like to get to know him better. Is he a local man?'

'Not him. Never seen him before. He looked like a man who could take care of himself, and he didn't want to talk when I tried to sound him out. He paid me for a couple of days feed and board and walked into the saloon. I stood watching him because he looks like the kind of man who needs to be watched.'

'I'd like to look at his horse,' Law said.

'Over here.' Smith raised the lantern and walked across to a stall on the far side of the barn. A big black horse rolled its eyes at them, wary of the lantern light, and Law patted its neck. He lifted the left foreleg to look at the shoe, and found it damaged in a way that had left the distinctive mark he had followed from DCL.

'This is the horse I trailed into town,' Law said. 'Can you tell me what the man was wearing? I want to be sure of his identity before I look him up. Getting him dead to rights is important.'

'Sure! He had a leather vest over a blue shirt and was wearing a black Stetson. I'd sure know him again; he's got a face you wouldn't wanta meet in a lonely place, and was a plumb unfriendly cuss.'

'You said he went into the saloon. Walk along there with me and point him out. I don't want to make a mistake.'

'All right. But what's this all about? You're the deputy marshal who's gonna clean up the county, ain't yuh? I heard you described. They say you're hell on wheels with a gun.'

'You can't believe all you're told,' Law replied.

They went along the sidewalk to the saloon and the ostler peered through a big front window to look at the throng of men inside the building.

'That's him,' he said excitedly. 'Him talking to that tall feller in the red shirt at the far end of the bar. He can't be mistaken. He's a tough-looking cuss.'

Law studied the man, recognizing him as the attacker who had been the only survivor of the six men he had shot it out with at DCL.

'Who is the man he's talking to?' Law asked. 'Do you know him?'

'Sure. Now he is a local man; Jake

Willard. He rides for Double C, and is a close friend of Leroy Cooper.'

Law thanked the ostler and the man slipped away into the darkness. Law paused for the merest instant, trying to work out what to do for the best. The man he had followed back from DCL looked like he was not going to move for hours, and had paid the ostler for at least a two-day stay in town. He had a hunch to stay with the man — watch his movements — and stood patiently at the window studying the interior of the saloon.

Fifteen minutes later he was relieved that he had guessed right, for the man drained his glass of beer, turned abruptly from the bar, and came to the batwings, looking as if he had a definite destination in mind. Law slid back into deeper shadow and waited. The man emerged from the saloon and paused on the sidewalk to light a cigarette before going on along the street. Law following silently, hoping for a break-through in his investigation.

Law was surprised when the man turned into Parker Strutt's office. He went to the lighted window and looked into the lawyer's room. Strutt was seated at his desk, and Law was further surprised when the newcomer confronted Strutt and began to speak long and earnestly. Strutt listened for some moments before interrupting, his eyes no longer shifty. He was gazing angrily at the man, and Law wished he could hear what was being said, but the window was closed and no sound emanated from the room.

Strutt got up from his desk and paced the office while the newcomer watched him sullenly. Law was surprised by the lawyer's change of attitude, and was tempted to walk into the office and join in the conversation. But he remained motionless, aware that he had to learn what he could, for there were questions in his mind he would put to Strutt at a later time. He faded into the shadows when Strutt's visitor turned to leave.

Strutt spoke sharply and the man paused in the doorway. Law waited, saw Strutt waggle a finger at the man before waving a dismissive hand, and he was back in the shadows when the man emerged and went along to the door of an eating-house.

Law was reminded of his own hunger but turned away when the man had ordered a meal. He went along to the law office, his mind teeming with conjecture. Joe Harmon was seated at the desk, writing reports, and the deputy looked up and grinned.

'You're soon back,' Harmon observed. 'Did you have any luck? Where's Jack? I need him to spell me while I take a break. I haven't had time to step outside the door since you left.'

Law frowned. 'Haven't you seen Julie Rutherford?' he countered. 'I told her to report to you soon as she reached town.'

Harmon shook his head. 'Like I said, I haven't left the office since you rode out. I've been kept pretty busy. The gal ain't been around. How'd you get on at DCL?'

Law explained in a low tone, and saw Harmon's expression change as the grim facts hit him. When Law explained about the survivor of the six attackers being in town, Harmon got to his feet.

'Let's pick him up,' he declared, 'and that lawyer, too. No sense letting them run around loose.'

'That's what I have in mind,' Law responded. 'We'll take the guy in the eating-house. I'll leave Strutt until later. I reckon to scare some truth out of him.'

Harmon picked up the jail keys and locked the street door when they left. They walked in silence to the eating-house, and Law led the way into the building, his right hand down at his side. He paused beside the table of the man he had been watching and drew his pistol. The man looked up, startled, his jaw working spasmodically on a mouthful of food.

'What's this?' he demanded, gazing

into the muzzle of Law's pistol.

'You're under arrest,' Law replied. 'Take his gun, Joe.'

Harmon moved to the man's side and disarmed him.

'On your feet,' Law directed, and the man arose, lifting his hands. 'What's your name?'

'Sam Hoyt. What's going on?'

'Hoyt, I'm arresting you for the murder of Jack Dawling, a deputy sheriff. You were with a party of riders who attacked the DCL ranch this afternoon.'

'Not me.' Hoyt shook his head. 'I just got into town from Mexico.'

'I followed you from DCL. We've got you dead to rights. Let's go along to the jail and talk about this, and don't waste my time trying to lie your way out of it because I saw you.'

Hoyt shrugged. Harmon led the way and they escorted their prisoner to the law office. Once inside, Hoyt refused to say anything further, and sat motionless under interrogation, shaking his head and denying all knowledge of the DCL ranch.

'Lock him in a cell, Joe,' Law said eventually, and remained in the background until Harmon had complied.

'I want to see a lawyer,' Hoyt called after them as they returned to the office. 'I ain't mixed up in anything.'

'I'll pick up Strutt now,' Law said. 'I'm gonna try and throw a scare into him before I bring him in. There's something about that little shyster I don't cotton to, and I got a feeling we'll learn a lot if I can scare him.'

He departed and walked along the street to Strutt's office, where a glance through the window showed him the lawyer still working at his desk. He entered the building.

Strutt's eyes began to shift when he looked up and saw Law standing in the doorway. His expression hardened and he leaned back in his seat, mouth gaping.

'What do you want, Marshal?' he demanded quickly. 'I don't have a lot of time to spare this evening. It might be better if you came back in the morning. I have to get some legal papers finished for the court.'

'You'll have to make time,' Law replied. 'I've been hearing some strange things about you, Strutt; strange because you're a lawyer. So we've got to have a talk to straighten out my doubts about you. Who was the man in here about fifteen minutes ago? He was big; wearing a blue shirt and a black Stetson. You had a lot to say to him and I want to know what it was about.'

Strutt seemed to sink into his seat. His hands fluttered as he interlaced his fingers across his small body.

'I don't know what you're talking about,' he said in a strangled tone. 'There's been no one in here since this morning. Who have you been talking to? Who has been telling lies about me?'

'You're the one telling lies.' Law walked to the desk and stood looking down at Strutt. He told the lawyer of his experience out at DCL and how he had tailed Hoyt back to town. 'So you see,' he said quietly. 'I saw Hoyt come into this office and watched the two of you. I reckon you were angry with him, probably because he failed to kill me out at DCL. I've arrested Hoyt, and he's asking to see you. But before we confront him I want you to tell me how you're mixed up in this crooked business.'

Strutt's hands were trembling, and Law could see that he was greatly troubled.

'If you're not too deeply involved you could help me with my investigation and it might count for you when you get to trial,' Law offered. 'You know how the law works, Strutt, so what about it?'

'I have nothing to say,' Strutt replied. 'You're wasting your time talking to me.'

'Then tell me who I ought to speak to. Don't make any mistake about it; the whole crooked business will come out into the open now I'm handling it. I reckon, when I finally pick up Chance Geest and Leroy Cooper, that I'll have enough evidence to work out what's been going on, but I want to know where you come into this, Strutt, and who else in town is mixed up in it.'

'Seth Geest was causing all the trouble,' Strutt said hesitantly. 'He was after Ben Rutherford for rustling Big G cattle.'

'Seth Geest might have been led to believe that Rutherford was guilty of rustling. I'm sure he believed that, but I don't think it happened that way. Rutherford had the blame shoved on to him to raise smoke which covered the real operation. All I have to do is uncover the motives of Geest and Rutherford and check on a few others, and I'm sure the truth will come out.'

'I didn't want to get mixed up in any of this,' Strutt said harshly. 'I said in the first place that it would get out of hand and murder would result. They said it wouldn't go that far, but it has, and now you're trying to blame me for what's happened.'

'Tell me the truth and I'll lay the blame where it belongs,' Law encouraged. 'I know you're mixed up in it so you've got nothing to lose and every-thing to gain. Some one is gonna hang for the murder of Dave Rutherford and Jack Dawling, and it won't be just the men who shot them. This is the only chance you'll have of pulling out, Strutt, so speak up.'

Strutt shook his head. His face was pale, his eyes narrowed, filled with fear. He lifted a hand to his forehead, his fingers trembling. Law moved to his left, intending to go to Strutt's side, intent on gaining something from the little man, but, even as he moved, the window overlooking the street shattered with heart-stopping suddenness and the heavy silence was blasted out by a volley of racketing shots.

Law hurled himself to the floor. Strutt gasped and fell back in his chair. Two bright splotches of blood had appeared as if by magic on his shirt front.

The shooting hammered on, and all Law could do was press himself to the floor and wait out the hellish storm.

8

Law angled the muzzle of his pistol at the lamp bracket across the room and sent a shot at the lamp, which flared and died. Darkness swept in but the shooting did not abate. The room was riddled with snarling bullets fired by several guns. The office was being torn apart by the rolling drumfire. Law's ears protested at the din. His Stetson was tugged by a passing slug and he pressed himself even closer to the floor, waiting for the lethal storm to pass.

He eased himself to the left, where a door led into the rear quarters of the building, and his outstretched left hand touched the door just as the shooting dwindled. He reached up, found the handle and opened the door, and was out of the office in a flash, aware that voices were shouting outside on the street.

He arose, gun in hand, and saw starlight showing at a window in the back wall. He felt around for an alley door, found it and unlocked it. As he jerked the door open a gun exploded in the alley and a slug crackled by his right ear. He ducked but kept moving forward and saw a man briefly illuminated in the flash of the shot. He triggered his pistol and the man went down.

Law ran out into the alley and sprinted along its length towards the back lots. His ears were ringing from the shooting, and he yawned in an attempt to clear them. There was shouting at his back, and then a gun boomed and he threw himself on the hard ground, slewing around the corner of the alley to take cover behind it. He got to his feet and fired two shots about waist high along the alley before moving away.

He was wondering who was out to get him. There were several men doing the shooting. He thought of Strutt, aware that the lawyer was dead, and a pang struck through him as he realized that he was up against an obdurate wall of mystery. Six men had attacked him at the DCL ranch and he had no idea who they were, even with Hoyt safely behind bars. And what had happened to Julie Rutherford? The girl seemed to have disappeared without a trace.

He turned into an alley and headed back to the street. Silence lay over the town, although his ears were still protesting at the shooting. He checked his pistol and reloaded spent chambers. A shadow moved to his right and he covered it.

'Who's there?' he called.

'Joe Harmon. Is that you, Law?'

'Yeah.'

'What in hell was all that shooting?' Harmon came out of the shadows, pistol in hand.

'I wish I knew.' Law explained what had happened. 'Cover me while I check out Strutt's office.'

He went along the street, checking

his surroundings ceaselessly. The street was deserted. No one had ventured out of doors to check on the shooting. Gun smoke hung in the air in front of Strutt's office. Law ventured to the broken front window and listened intently. No sound emanated from the darkness.

'Joe, get a lamp and bring it over here,' he called.

'Be right with you.' Harmon dropped back to the saloon, pushed through the batwings and picked up a lamp. He came along the sidewalk, holding the lamp aloft, and Law covered him, gazing into the surrounding shadows.

Harmon walked into the lawyer's office, his pistol in his right hand. Law followed closely, ready for action, and they stood before Strutt's desk looking around at the bullet-shattered room. Strutt was slumped in his chair. Blood had soaked the front of his shirt. His mouth was agape; eyes steady now, staring at them from beyond the divide that separated life from death.

'Did you learn anything from him before the shooting started?' Harmon asked.

Law shook his head. 'He wasn't saying anything. Let's check out the place. I left the alley door open when I got out. We'll close up until morning.'

Harmon walked through to the back room and, as lamplight chased out the shadows, he uttered an exclamation of shock and halted quickly. Law almost walked into the deputy's big figure, but side-stepped at the last moment. He saw a figure seated in a chair in a corner of the room, and shock struck him hard when he recognized Julie Rutherford. The girl, bound hand and foot to the chair, had a neckerchief stuffed into her mouth. She was struggling against her bonds, her eyes wide with shock.

Law hurried forward and released her. She sprang to her feet but slumped, and Law grabbed her, holding her upright.

'What happened to you?' he demanded.

173

'How'd you come to be tied up in here?'

'I met Leroy Cooper on my way to town,' she replied bitterly. 'He rode with me, talking mainly about Dave, until we arrived, and then he drew his gun and threatened me. I had to go along with him. He brought me across the back lots and into this room. Parker Strutt came in and spoke to me. I told him about the trouble at DCL and Strutt told Leroy I had to be killed. Leroy didn't want any part of that and left me here tied up, and I have no doubt what would have happened if you hadn't found me.'

'Strutt is dead,' Law mused. 'It looks like I need to talk to Leroy now, and mighty quick. Did he say anything that might give us some idea what he was up to?'

'I asked him if he knew who killed Dave and he said he didn't. When I was brought in here, I remember Strutt saying he was waiting for some men to show up who would help them, but he didn't mention any names. Leroy said it was over and he wasn't going to stick around. They had a big argument about that before Leroy left.'

'I've had it in the back of my mind that Leroy and Chance Geest had something to do with the trouble around here.' Law was considering the impressions he had gained since arriving. 'Have you any idea where Chance is staying these days? Seth Geest told me his son was living with a woman on a ranch west of town. Have you heard anything?'

Julie shook her head. 'I've seen him talking in town to Emma Took, whose father, Frank, owns the FT spread five miles out on the trail to Sunset Creek.'

'That will do to be going on with.' Law took the girl's arm. 'Come on. Let's get you to the hotel and bedded down for the night. Stick close to the hotel until I show up again, huh?'

Julie allowed herself to be led away without protest. Law took her to the hotel and saw her safely inside. Harmon went off on a round of the town and

Law went back to the jail to confront Seth Geest.

'What was all that shooting about?' asked Geest.

'Are you concerned that your son was involved in it?' Law countered.

'What are you getting at? Chance is law-abiding, like me. He was trying to set up a cattle business when the rustlers struck. Him and his pards were the first to be wiped out. They lost everything.'

'I heard there was bad blood between Chance and Dave Rutherford.'

'Don't try to pin Dave's murder on Chance,' Seth growled. 'You're looking in the wrong direction, Marshal.'

'Maybe, and maybe not. Give me some facts I can work on and perhaps I'll get to the bottom of what's going on here. You've caused enough trouble on your own. Men have been killed on your say-so. If you are not guilty of anything then why did you start riding rough-shod over your neighbour?'

'I told you, I got proof of Ben

Rutherford's guilt.'

'Yeah. Well I'll be looking into that side of it later. I've got to stop the shooting and killing before I can get down to the finer points of law dealing.'

Geest turned away and sat down on the end of his bunk. Law moved on to Scar Crowley's cell. The big ex-deputy was stretched out on his back, his hands behind his head. He regarded Law without changing his expression, his thick lips pulled into a wry smile.

'Dave Rutherford's murder,' Law said. 'Tell me about it again.'

'No chance. I told you all I know, which is nothing. It wouldn't do any good to champ on it again. You're up the creek, Marshal, and there ain't no way you can get to what was going on around here.'

Law gave it up as a bad job and went back into the office. He sat down at the desk and read the report Harmon had written since taking over, finding nothing in the deputy's words to help the case along. The street door was opened and Law drew his gun as a big figure stepped into the office. He relaxed when he recognized Grat Kibbee. The banker came to the desk, his face showing shock.

'I just heard that Parker was killed in his office, Marshal. What happened?'

Law pointed to a seat and Kibbee dropped heavily into it. He was sweating and there was a hunted expression on his face. Law explained what had happened, and Kibbee's expression deepened when he learned about Julie Rutherford being held prisoner in Strutt's back office.

'From what I've heard, you were pretty close to Strutt,' Law said. 'So tell me what was going on. What was he mixed up in?'

'If he was caught up in any crookedness, I knew nothing about it,' Kibbee asserted. 'I can't believe he'd be so stupid, unless he took part under threat.'

'Have you been threatened in the same way?' Law demanded.

'I've been concerned for weeks that a hold-up gang will ride in and rob the bank.'

'You were pretty close to Strutt, huh?'

'Yes. We did a lot of business together. I could see he was under a big strain, but I had no idea what was on his mind.'

'I will get to the bottom of it.' Law spoke firmly. 'I'd like to talk to you again, probably tomorrow, after you've had time to reflect on the past few days.'

'I wish I could help you.' Kibbee got to his feet, shaking his head, and went to the door, where he paused. 'If there's anything I can do then don't hesitate to call on me,' he offered.

Law nodded and looked down at the report he had been reading. Kibbee opened the door to depart, and Leroy Cooper and Chance Geest appeared in the doorway as if they had been waiting for the door to open. Both were holding pistols, and Cooper struck Kibbee on the head with the barrel of his gun. Kibbee fell to the floor with an impact that shook the office. Law looked up, his right hand instinctively reaching for his gun, but he froze under the menace of two levelled pistols covering him.

'That's right,' Leroy Cooper snarled. 'Sit still, and get your hands up. You so much as blink and you're dead.'

Law raised his hands, his eyes narrowed and watchful. Cooper kicked the inert banker as he crossed the threshold, and Law's eyes narrowed when there was no reaction from Kibbee.

'I've been hoping to see you, Chance,' Law said softly. 'I've got it figured that you and Leroy know a lot about what's been going on around here.'

'So I've saved you the trouble of hunting me.' Geest waggled his gun. 'Check him for hardware, Leroy, and then let's turn my pa loose.'

Cooper approached Law and snatched away the marshal's deadly gun.

'What was going on at Strutt's

office, Leroy?' Law demanded. 'Why did you take Julie Rutherford in there? Who forced Strutt to work against the law? And who murdered Dave Rutherford?'

'Just shut your mouth and get my pa out of the cells,' Geest said roughly. 'We'll take you along with us, Marshal, and maybe the men we're working with will give you some answers.' He laughed harshly. 'More likely they'll shoot you like a dog. Go on, get moving.'

Law picked up the keys and entered the cell block, followed closely by his captors.

'Unlock all the cells,' Chance directed.

Law unlocked the door of Seth Geest's cell and the Big G rancher moved into the open doorway, frowning as he took in the situation.

'What's going on, Chance?' he demanded. His frown deepened at the unusual sight of Law standing with his hands shoulder high, covered by two guns. 'Son, you won't get away with this.'

'We are getting away with it,' Chance replied. 'Don't give me a hard time, Pa. You don't belong behind bars so I'm turning you loose.'

'No.' Seth shook his head stubbornly. 'I've had time to think while I've been in here. I didn't like the deal we got at the time, and there's been killing done when I said I wouldn't go along with it if they started that. Where do you think it's all going to end? Look at you now. You've disarmed a marshal and you're holding him prisoner in his own jail, and it won't stop there. You've got it all wrong, Chance. There's no future in this, and I ain't stirring out of this cell.'

Seth turned and slammed the door to, the clang ringing through the cell block. The rancher sat down on the end of his bunk and folded his arms, his expression like that of a mule that had decided to quit. Law was watching Chance and Leroy closely. Chance's face was a picture of shock and amazement. He stared at his father, shaking his head as he tried to come to terms with the situation.

'You can't stay in here, Pa,' he urged. 'They'll put a rope around your neck for sure. Stop fooling around and come on. We got horses outside. Let's get going before it's too late.'

'I ain't running.' Seth shook his head. 'I ain't done a blame thing wrong and I ain't gonna act like I did. That bunch of gunnies that got stuck on me — I never hired them — Bassell, Tog Doughty, Hap Jones — they were border scum sent in to do Butch Rainey's dirty work.'

'They only did what you told them,' Chance argued.

'I didn't want no one killed. I said that, and they agreed. I ain't moving, and you and Leroy better think about your own position. Quit while you can. If you go on from here you'll be branded outlaws, and that can have only one ending. Pull out of it while you still can.'

'Let's get out of here,' Leroy said. 'No use arguing with the old coot if he's set his mind on staying. I always said it would be a mistake to take him in with us.'

'He wouldn't have got wind of the business if you'd kept your big mouth shut,' Chance retorted. 'But he's my pa and I ain't leaving him behind bars, so that's that. He's going with us.'

'Or what?' Leroy demanded. 'If he don't wanta go then he don't wanta go. You can't make him. Let's up stakes before we get more problems. We're standing in the jail arguing because your pa is loco and oughta be locked up. Well, you do what you want, Chance. Me, I'm getting outa here.'

'Not without Pa!' Chance insisted.

Law was ready to grab any advantage that came his way. His mind was intent on what had been said. The name of Butch Rainey interested him, and filled in a number of gaps in his thoughts. He watched Leroy scowling at Chance, and saw that the two men were now covering each other with their pistols.

'He ain't gonna come unless you

carry him,' Leroy insisted. 'Let's get moving. If he wants to stay here then let him.'

'Nobody is going anywhere,' Joe Harmon said from the doorway of the office. 'Drop those guns and throw up your hands.'

Law's head jerked round and he gazed at Harmon, whose pistol was levelled at the hip. Chance and Leroy froze for the merest second, but Law moved instantly. He slammed his left fist against Chance's jaw and grabbed at the man's pistol as Chance buckled at the knees. Leroy fired at Harmon, who staggered and spun away, and by the time Leroy could switch his attention to Law, the marshal had reversed his grip on Chance's gun and was ready to fight.

The cell block reverberated to the quick blast of gunfire. Leroy took Law's first shot in the chest and pitched backwards, his gun falling from his slackening grasp. Gun smoke rasped in Law's throat as he breathed deeply, but the action was over. Blood was seeping across Leroy's shirt front. Chance, dazed by Law's quick punch, was helpless on the floor, gazing up at Law like a pole-axed steer in a slaughter-house.

Law slammed and locked the door of Seth Geest's cell. He unlocked another cell and motioned for Chance to enter it. Chance arose and staggered in through the doorway, and the door clanged to behind him. Law picked up Leroy's gun and stuck it into the back of his belt. He bent over Leroy to check him, and shook his head, for it was obvious that Leroy was heading down that long, one-way trail to Boot Hill. He grasped Leroy's collar and dragged the youngster into the law office, then closed and locked the connecting door between office and cells.

Joe Harmon was leaning against the office wall beside the door. Blood was spreading through the fabric of his shirt, and he shook his head when he met Law's steady gaze.

'It ain't too bad,' he remarked. 'Busted my shoulder but missed the lung. I reckon I'll be out of action for a month. What was going on? I came back to the office to find Kibbee stretched out on the floor and that confrontation going on in the cells. Where did Chance and Leroy come from?'

'They were skulking around town, I suspect. They came to bust Seth free but he wouldn't leave with them, and I learned one or two interesting things from what was said. The hard cases I've been fighting around here are from Butch Rainey's border gang of rustlers.'

Doc Rouse appeared in the doorway, his medical bag in hand. He uttered an ejaculation when he saw Kibbee on the threshold, bent over the banker, and then shook his head. He had a cursory glance at Leroy and went on to Harmon. Law dropped to one knee beside Leroy, who was barely conscious.

'I'm sorry it came to this for you, Leroy,' Law said softly.

'Go to hell!' Leroy hissed. 'I took my

187

chance and it went flat on me. I ain't sorry.'

'Who killed Dave Rutherford?' Law asked.

'I don't know. I didn't do it so don't put the blame on me. I thought Chance did it, but he wouldn't admit it when I asked him. Is Chance dead?'

'No. He's locked in a cell now. You ain't got long, Leroy. Is there anything you want me to tell your pa? I'll send word to him soon as I can.'

Leroy shook his head. He was finding it hard to breathe. 'Pa and me rode our separate ways a long time ago. I guess it's too late for talk.'

He fell silent, his eyes closing and then he relaxed muscle by muscle, his harsh breathing sighing away to nothing. Law straightened, shaking his head. He went to the inert figure of Grat Kibbee lying on the threshold where he had fallen after being struck by Leroy Cooper, and was shocked to find the banker dead, his skull broken by the pistol blow.

The street door opened and Bill Baylin, the night jailer, entered, shotgun tucked under his right elbow. He looked at the bodies on the floor and then walked to the desk.

'Looks like you've been busy,' he observed. 'I heard the shooting, and that's why I'm early for duty. I got a feeling it is gonna be a long night.'

'We'll get started when Doc has finished,' Law said. 'If I can get the truth out of some of our prisoners then I'll be ready to ride out in the morning on the clean-up trail.'

'I'll take Joe along to my office and finish him off there,' Doc Rouse said at length. 'He won't be back on duty inside of a month. That's the best I can do. Have you got any other customers needing my attention?'

'Not at the moment,' Law replied, 'but I reckon there will be more, a lot more, before this is done.'

Rouse departed with Harmon, and Law pointed to the cell keys lying on a corner of the desk.

'Bring Seth Geest out here, Bill,' he said. 'He's had a change of heart and I wanta question him before he changes his mind again.'

Baylin disappeared into the cell block to emerge moments later behind Seth Geest. The G Bar rancher came to the desk shaking his head, and Law braced himself for a hard time. He waited until Geest was seated before asking questions, and was pleasantly surprised when the rancher nodded.

'I've decided to come clean, Marshal,' Geest said firmly. 'I was a fool to fall for the talk I got but I've come to my senses, and I don't want a deal from you. I'll tell you what I know and you make what you can from it.'

'So start at the beginning and explain how you came to get into such a fix,' Law urged.

'Greed, I reckon. Chance wanted to get on — run his own place — and I never had enough dough to help him. When I told him I couldn't come up with the cash he needed he robbed the stage coach — him and Leroy — and was recognized by Sim Wenn the coach driver, who told Scar Crowley. Instead of arresting them, Crowley did a deal, and Wenn was killed to close his mouth. I couldn't say anything about what I knew because my boy was involved.'

Geest broke off and moved impatiently before resuming.

'Before I could decide what to do about the situation, Crowley came out to the ranch and talked. He knew some rustlers who wanted to move in and clean out the entire range. I could go in with them, or get wiped out by them. It was a no-win situation and, with Chance just setting up on his own, I went along with Crowley. The next thing I knew there were hard cases on my payroll and Ben Rutherford was made to look like he'd rustled my stock. I didn't have any say in the business. They used me and my place as a headquarters for rustling, and they would have killed me if I hadn't gone along with them.'

'I'll want all this down in writing soon as I can get around to it,' Law said. 'Tell me about Scar Crowley. He looks like a man who figures on a wanted dodger, but I can't place him at the moment.'

'I don't know anything about him.' Geest shook his head. 'All I can tell you is that he was mighty familiar with those border rustlers, throwing out orders to them, and they didn't argue with him. They would have killed their own mothers if he'd told them to.'

'Do you know anything about Dave Rutherford's murder?' Law asked.

Seth shook his head. 'Not a thing,' he said.

Law was thoughtful while Baylin returned Geest to his cell. He was impatient to make a breakthrough in this case, but was handicapped by being on his own. He could not leave the jail with so many prisoners in it, and decided to send to Sheriff Derry for more help. The street door opened at that moment and Julie Rutherford entered, apparently in some considerable distress, for she tripped over Kibbee's inert body as if she did not see it on the threshold, and fell heavily.

Law sprang to his feet and hurried to her side, his keen eyes having seen a smear of blood on her face.

9

Julie was so badly shocked she could barely stand alone when Law raised her up. The blood on her forehead was seeping from a large bruise. Her eyes were filled with bewilderment and her hands were trembling.

'My father!' she gasped. 'Two men came into the hotel and took him. I tried to stop them but one of them hit me with his pistol. When I came to my senses, Pa was gone.'

'Wait in here while I investigate.' Law motioned to Baylin. 'Keep an eye on things until I get back, Bill,' he said.

He hurried out to the street, pausing only to hear the jail door being locked behind him, and then went along to the hotel. The building seemed deserted, and he stood in the lobby, wondering where to start looking for Ben Rutherford. He went back to the street and peered around into the shadows. The town was quiet — too quiet, he mused. He went along the sidewalk to the livery barn, drawing his pistol as he entered. The place was in darkness, and he crossed to the office, where a lantern burned.

When he saw the liveryman tied in his chair, with a cloth stuffed into his mouth, he hurried forward and released the man.

'Three men jumped me,' Tom Smith gasped. 'Then two of them went into town. They came back shortly with Ben Rutherford, piled him into a saddle and rode out. I never heard a word spoken between them. They were hard cases who knew what they were doing, and they sure didn't waste any time.'

'Did you get a look at their horses?' Law asked.

Smith shook his head. 'I was here in the office all the time. They tied me up first thing. I heard them leave, but I didn't see anything. I don't know what this town is coming to. I was up in

Abilene in the bad old days, but this place is getting to be worse.'

'I'm gonna have to wait until morning before I can follow tracks,' Law mused. 'You saw the men who took Ben Rutherford. Would you know any of them again? Could you identify them?'

'I don't think so. They took me by surprise, and I was scared as hell they would kill me. I didn't notice any details.'

Law departed and walked back to the jail, aware that he could do nothing until daylight. Baylin let him into the jail, and Law was relieved when he saw that Kibbee and Leroy Cooper had been removed. He questioned Julie again, but the girl could add nothing to what she had already told him.

'The two men who took your father,' Law urged. 'Had you ever seen them before?'

'No. They were strangers.'

'Would you know either of them again? Can you describe either of them?'

'I'd know the one who hit me.' Julie

shivered. 'He was big, running to fat, and his face was greasy. He wheezed when he breathed, and there was something wrong with his right eye. It didn't look normal. His left eye was brown, but the right one was milky. I think it was blind.'

'That's something, anyway,' Law mused. 'How was he dressed?'

'Brown shirt, black pants, and a black Stetson. That's all I can remember.'

'I'll be out on the trail first thing in the morning,' Law said. 'I think you should go back to the hotel and try to get some sleep.'

'Let me ride with you tomorrow,' she pleaded. 'You'll need a witness with you if you come up with those men.'

'I'll think about it,' Law promised.

Julie got to her feet and Law escorted her to the hotel, saw her safely into her room, and then went back to the jail. He went through to the cells and confronted Seth Geest, aware that all his other prisoners were listening attentively to his questioning. But Geest had nothing more to add to his statement, and Law moved on to the door of Scar Crowley's cell.

'I've been learning a lot about you, Crowley,' he said. 'So you're tied up with Butch Rainey and his wide-loopers.'

'Who is Butch Rainey?' Crowley countered, grinning. 'I've never heard of him.'

Returning to the office, Law sat at the desk and considered the situation. He had come into this county to sort out a local problem, but it was obvious now that the trouble he found was not local. He was certain now that the big rustling gangs were involved, and he had been up against their men rather than hard cases hired by Geest or the local ranchers.

He accepted the idea, and realized that he had to push on with locating Ben Rutherford, for the rancher's kidnapping was obviously another move by the rustlers. He talked to Bill Baylin, questioning the jailer closely on events that had occurred previously in the county, but learned nothing significant. There had been practically no trouble in the county before Dave Rutherford was murdered. Seth Geest had talked about being rustled, and finally accused Ben Rutherford of stealing his stock. The only other thing that had been wrong, Baylin was certain, was the local stage coach had been robbed.

'I'm gonna turn in and get some sleep,' Law said eventually. 'I'll need to be up and running early in the morning.'

'I can handle this end of the deal,' Baylin replied, sitting down at the desk when Law arose. 'There's a cot in a back room you can use for sleeping. You'll be on hand, and I'll call you if you're needed. You look like you ain't closed your eyes since you hit this town.'

Law nodded and went into the back room. He removed his gun belt, stretched out on the cot and, moments later, was asleep, to be awakened about two hours later by a rough hand shaking his shoulder. He opened his eyes and looked up into the intent face of Bill Baylin.

'Sorry to disturb you, Marshal, but there's a man in the office who reckons he's got news for you.'

Law arose, buckled on his gunbelt, and followed the jailer into the office. Darkness was pressing in against the big window overlooking the street and he blinked tiredly as he turned to the newcomer standing beside the desk.

'Mike Layton!' he gasped, recognizing a colleague from Amarillo. 'What brings you here?'

'Jed. How you doing?' Layton was tall and lean, no more than twenty-five, and his serious eyes crinkled as he smiled. 'I'm on my way to meet up with the Rangers down on the border, and I've got some information you'll need. The Rangers have been working hand in hand with the Rurales across the border, and they've got the Butch Rainey gang and his Mexican rustler pards on the run. What's been happening around here is all part of Rainey's last big cattle steal before his gang moves on to new pastures, if they can slip through our net.'

'Give me the details. I've had my hands full around here, but, for the moment, I've shot my way through the opposition. I've got one trail to follow in the morning. But I've had the feeling all along that I was up against Rainey's gang.'

'Here are some new wanted dodgers they put together in Amarillo. You better check to see if you've already taken care of some of them.'

Law picked up the thin sheaf of papers Layton placed on the desk, and was filled with sudden excitement as he scanned the collection of faces and descriptions. Almost immediately he came across a likeness of Scar Crowley, and showed the dodger to Layton.

'This one I got behind bars right now,' he said. 'He was the deputy sheriff here when I arrived.'

He continued looking through the dodgers, and found Sam Hoyt staring up at him.

'This one is also behind bars,' he said. 'He led five men against me out at DCL. So I'm on the right track. I've been fighting Rainey's bunch and didn't know it. This gives me an edge, Mike.'

'I wish I could stay and help you clean up but I have to be in Douro soon as I can make it, and I got to be splitting the breeze.' Layton turned to the door. 'Watch out for trouble around here. There's no telling where Rainey's gang will try to break out. So long, Jed.'

Law followed his colleague out to the street. They shook hands, and then Layton swung into his saddle and turned away. His horse was running within a few paces, and he vanished into the shadows and was gone. Law stood motionless until all sounds had faded, and then went back into the office and locked the door.

Bill Baylin was looking at the

dodgers, and grinned when he looked up at Law.

'They got Crowley dead to rights. He's a rustler, huh? And he's been deputy sheriff around here. No wonder the bad men have been doing just what they like. And who else was mixed up with that gang? Kibbee and Strutt are dead — two of the most prominent men in town. Were they mixed up with the rustlers?'

'That is something we have to find out.' Law motioned to the cell keys on a corner of the desk. 'Bring Crowley out here and we'll see if he'll change his tune now.'

Baylin went into the cells and returned a moment later with Scar Crowley, who sat down in front of the desk and gazed impassively at Law. The dozen or so dodgers were lying face-upwards on the desk.

'Take a look at these, Crowley,' Law said. 'Is there any face here you can recognize?'

'I don't know any of them,' Crowley

replied. 'I can't help you.'

'You must recognize this one.' Law pointed to the drawing of Crowley's face, and had the satisfaction of seeing shock crowd into the man's heavy features. He grinned. 'It looks like I've caught up with you, huh?'

Crowley shook his head. 'I got nothing to say.'

'You'd better start getting wise to the situation. Rainey and the gang are trapped by Texas Rangers, and the Rurales have got Rainey's Mexican pards in a tight spot across the border. It's all over for that crooked bunch, which includes you. There'll be a hanging session for the murders that have been committed, and there's no telling where the guilt will fall when frightened men start talking. You've been right in the middle of the killings around here, and it ain't looking good for you. So start spilling what you know and you might save your neck.'

Crowley looked fixedly into Law's hard gaze, and didn't like what he saw.

'I'm open to a deal,' he said at length.

'What have you got to offer?' Law countered.

'You want Dave Rutherford's killer, huh? The deal is, I walk free if I give you the guilty man.'

'If I arrest the proven killer on your say-so then I'll clear you on any charges except murder,' Law offered.

'I ain't murdered anybody,' Crowley said. 'I set up the rustling around here for Rainey, and he sent in some of the gang, who did the killings — men like Hawk Bassell, Tog Doughty, Hap Jones and Sam Hoyt.'

'I've got Hoyt dead to rights for Jack Dawling's death,' Law said. 'So let's get down to Dave Rutherford's murder. He was shot in the back at close range by someone using a derringer, so Doc said.'

'That gun ain't a million miles away from here,' Crowley said tersely. 'I picked it up in the DCL yard when I went to look at Dave's body. Strutt came into town with the news of Dave's death after he and Kibbee rode out to DCL. Strutt and Kibbee had been threatened into helping the gang. Strutt was doing legal work to enable Rainey to take over some of the cattle spreads around here, and Kibbee was supplying figures to prove Rainey was paying good money for the ranches. Nobody was gonna get paid, but that is how Rainey operates.'

'So who killed Dave Rutherford?' Law pressed.

'You got the killer behind bars right now.' Crowley fell silent for a moment, his eyes filled with a calculating glitter. 'Do I have a deal with you over this? If you get the evidence against the killer, I walk free?'

'If you're not involved in any murders yourself,' Law insisted.

'Chance Geest shot Dave in the back. Chance and Leroy Cooper were riding for Rainey. They went into DCL with Dave Rutherford; found they couldn't make it, so they turned to rustling. The trouble is nobody steals cows in the area where Rainey works, so Rainey caught them cold but took them into the gang. The trouble was, Dave Rutherford wouldn't go along with that. He knew Rainey was after the Circle R and he didn't like it. He had a bad fight with Chance over it, and Chance bided his time until he could kill Dave. I got this from Chance himself. He knew I was Rainey's eyes and ears in the county.'

Crowley leaned back in his seat, his forehead beaded with sweat.

'That's it,' he said. 'Chance Geest shot Dave in the back because Dave wouldn't go along with the rustling. The murder weapon is in the bottom righthand drawer of the desk.'

Law jerked open the drawer, picked up a .41 derringer, and laid it on the desk top.

'That's it,' Crowley said. 'The gun that killed Dave Rutherford. You can prove it belongs to Chance by talking to Abe Fremont about it. Fremont owns the gun shop in town, and he had trouble getting his money for it when he sold it to Chance last year.'

'I'll check out your story,' Law said. 'If you're right about Chance then I'll clear you.'

'I believe you,' Crowley said. He got to his feet and turned to the cell block.

Baylin looked at Law. 'Have you finished with him?' he asked.

'Yeah. Lock him up, and bring Chance Geest out here.'

Baylin jangled the bunch of keys as he escorted Crowley back to the cells, and returned a moment later with Chance Geest.

'Sit down, Chance,' Law said. 'You can help me clear up Dave's murder.'

'You ain't gonna pin that on me,' Chance said sullenly, sliding into the chair that Crowley had vacated. He looked apprehensive.

'I'm not gonna try and pin it on anyone,' Law replied. 'I aim to get at the truth, and as you were one of Dave's partners, and you'd had a bad fight with him, it stands to reason that I want to get your side of what happened. So don't get a chip on your shoulder about this. Let's try and sort it out, huh?'

Chance grimaced. 'It looks like you've got a tight hold on the rustlers,' he mused. 'My pa ain't guilty of anything. They would have killed him if he hadn't gone along with them.'

'Your pa has got good sense. He's told me the truth about what was happening around here, and I'll check out his statement. So why don't you do the same and give me the low-down on what's been happening? I know you and Leroy have been rustling for Rainey, and Dave Rutherford was against that so you had a fight with him. The next thing, Dave is shot in the back out at DCL.'

'Leroy did it.' Chance moistened his lips. 'I was there with him. We tried to talk Dave round to our way of thinking but he couldn't be swayed, so Leroy shot him.'

'It's easy to say Leroy did it, because

he's dead and can't deny it,' Law observed.

'I'm giving you the truth. I was there and I saw it happen. Leroy did it.'

'With your derringer?' Law picked up the small pistol. 'You bought this last year from Abe Fremont's gun store.'

'Yeah. I feel bad about that. Leroy knew I was carrying the derringer. When Dave turned away in the yard he said he was gonna head for Spanish Creek and spill the beans to Sheriff Derry. Leroy snatched the derringer from my pocket and let Dave have it between the shoulder blades. Whether you believe it or not, that's the truth of it.'

Law studied Chance's intent face, aware that he might never get at the truth of the murder. He nodded.

'I'll take a statement from you later,' he said. 'Leroy kidnapped Julie Rutherford this afternoon and took her to Strutt's office, where I found her hog-tied in a back room there. Strutt wanted no part of kidnapping and the next thing, he's shot dead in his office. I suspect you and Leroy had something to do with that. You were getting in over your heads with Rainey's bunch and were trying to get out of it. You and Leroy killed Strutt, and when you came in here and found Kibbee talking to me, Leroy killed Kibbee.'

'Remember Leroy did it, not me,' Chance pointed out. 'Sure, we attacked Strutt's office. We saw you going in there, and we knew Strutt would spill his guts the minute you put pressure on him. Leroy opened fire through Strutt's window, and his first shots hit Strutt. Then you shot out the light and we pulled out.'

'Who robbed the stage coach?' Law demanded.

'Leroy and Dave.' Chance grinned. 'I can see you don't believe me, but that's the truth.'

Law motioned to the watchful Baylin. 'Put him back in his cell,' he said. 'We'll get a statement from him tomorrow.'

Chance returned to the cell block

and Law leaned back in his seat. He was reasonably certain that he had covered most of the questions in his mind, although he doubted that he had heard the full truth from Chance Geest, but more questioning might reveal that truth and, for the moment, he was satisfied.

He sat motionless at the desk until dawn showed at the window and, when sunlight chased away the shadows of the night, he arose, stretched tiredly, and left the office to get breakfast and then to begin his hunt for Ben Rutherford.

The hotel lobby was deserted when Law reached it, and he peered into the small dining-room, hoping to see Julie Rutherford there, but the place was empty and he went to the reception desk and rang the bell. A woman appeared in the doorway of a back room and looked questioningly at him.

'I'm looking for Julie Rutherford,' Law said.

'She's not here,' the woman replied.

'She left an hour before dawn. Said she was going out to Circle R. Her father was kidnapped last night and she said she thought the men who took him had ridden out to the ranch.'

Law bit his lip on an oath and turned on his heel. He left the saloon at a run and headed for the stable. The last thing he wanted was Julie Rutherford out alone on the range.

A gun blasted from the loft door of the stable, which was situated above the big door fronting the street, and Law felt the smash of a bullet in the flesh of his left thigh. He fell into the dust of the street, but even so, his pistol was cocked in his hand as he made contact with the hard ground. He saw gun smoke drifting from the loft doorway, caught a glimpse of a dark shadow moving back from the door aperture, and fired two quick shots before rolling over a couple of times.

By the time he got back into the aim, a man had sprawled forward in the doorway and lay with his head and left arm dangling in space. Law pushed himself to his feet, gun ready and, clenching his teeth against the pain in his leg, ran forward to the stable, ears ringing from the crash of the shots. He hurled himself recklessly into the barn, ready for anything.

10

Law ran headlong into the barn and halted, swinging his gun as he searched the gloomy interior. He made for the loft ladder and, ignoring the pain in his left thigh, surged upwards until he could cover the man he had shot in the loft doorway. He halted near the top of the ladder, for the man had not moved since falling, and then he went up and checked the inert figure. The man was a stranger, and he was dead.

Peering through the open doorway at the street, Law caught a glimpse of three riders loping past the front of the barn and called a challenge. The trio glanced up at him and immediately drew their pistols. Law dropped flat as shots hammered, and returned fire. One of the riders pitched out of his saddle and lay crumpled in the dust of the street. The remaining two galloped to the right out of Law's sight.

Law descended the ladder and dashed out of the barn. He peered along the street and saw two horses standing at the hitching rail in front of the bank. There was no sign of the riders. He moved out to where the crumpled figure was lying and examined it. The man was dead. He went back to the sidewalk and advanced towards the horses.

In the back of his mind, Law was wondering about Julie Rutherford. He had been about to saddle and ride out to Circle R in search of her, but now he knew he could not leave town with only Bill Baylin in the jail guarding the prisoners. He halted in the doorway of the general store and looked around for the two men. The town was still, seemingly deserted, and an ominous silence reigned. He assumed the trio of riders were more of Rainey's hard cases, and turned quickly and went through the store to the back, wanting to catch up with the two men before further trouble developed.

He left the building by the rear door and checked the back lots, but saw nothing suspicious and hurried towards the jail, gaining the alley beside it without incident. Moving to the street end of the alley, he checked for the two men, saw no sign of them, and moved quickly to the front door of the office.

'Bill,' he called urgently. 'Let me in.'

The office door was unlocked and Baylin peered out, a shotgun in his hands. 'What's going on?' he demanded. 'What was that shooting?'

Law explained as he entered the office and Baylin slammed and locked the door.

'I was getting a mite concerned,' Baylin said. 'What do you reckon is going on?'

'I don't know yet, but I mean to find out. Let's check on the prisoners.'

Baylin picked up the cell keys and led the way into the cell block. Law reloaded the spent chambers in his pistol and looked around at the cells.

Crowley was in a cell which had a window overlooking the alley at the side of the jail, and the ex-deputy was in the act of turning away from the window.

'Is someone out there?' Law demanded, and ran to the back door. He unbolted the heavy door and jerked it open, but when he looked around the alley it was deserted. He walked to the window that gave light to the cell block and checked the dust but was unable to see any footprints. He went to the rear of the alley and gazed around the back lots, then shook his head and returned to the jail, holstering his pistol as he did so.

When he entered the cells, Law saw Baylin standing with his hands raised at shoulder height; his shotgun was lying on the floor at his feet. Scar Crowley was at the door of his cell, right hand thrust between the bars, holding a levelled pistol.

'Just stand still,' Crowley said hoarsely. 'All I wanta do is get outa here. There ain't no sense anyone getting himself killed over this. Just do like I say and nobody will get hurt. I'm leaving this joint and I'm taking these prisoners with me.'

'You won't get away with this,' Law warned. 'Where did you get the gun from?'

'A kind friend passed it through the window.' Crowley grinned. 'Get your hands up, Marshal. If you reach for your gun I'll kill you pretty damn quick. I ain't taking a chance with you. Get your hands up. Baylin, open the cells. I'll start shooting if you so much as blink. Have you got that?'

'I ain't going anywhere,' Seth Geest rasped. 'I don't want any part of this, Crowley. I'm through taking orders from you.'

'You'll do like I say. We're getting outa here. Come on, Baylin, get this door open.'

'Don't do it, Bill,' Law said urgently. 'He's got the gun, but he can't get out if we don't open that door. It's a Mexican stand-off, and he can't win nohow.'

'I can kill one of you,' Crowley rasped, 'and I don't care which one.'

The muzzle of the gun he was holding had not wavered from covering Law, who was watching intently for the slightest lapse of concentration by Crowley. The ex-deputy had not disarmed Law, probably because he feared Law's great speed of draw, and Law was tensed ready to take advantage of the situation.

'I don't know why you're doing this,' Law said softly. 'If you shoot either of us you'll be wanted for murder, and yet you have a chance of walking out of here a free man once I've checked your statement.'

'I'd rather get out of here by my own efforts than rely on your word,' Crowley said. 'Come on, Baylin, you're wasting time. I want out of here now.'

Law was watching Crowley's gun hand. The man's trigger finger was curved around the trigger, his knuckle showing white under the pressure being applied. Law knew he was standing in the gateway to hell, and was prepared for a desperate grab for his own gun, but Crowley was watching him intently, only too aware of the marshal's prowess with a gun.

'I'll let you out,' Baylin said reluctantly. 'We don't want any shooting in here.'

He advanced to the door of Crowley's cell, jangling the big bunch of keys in his right hand.

'Don't get between me and the marshal,' Crowley warned. 'I'll kill the pair of you if I have to.'

Baylin moved in sideways, his right hand extended to put the key of the door into the lock. Crowley's eyes glittered as he gazed at Law, his gun steady as a rock in his right hand. Baylin remained out of the line of fire. He fumbled with the key, causing it to grate against obdurate metal as if he were having trouble finding the key-hole. Law watched with bated breath, the fingers of his right hand tingling as he looked for a life or death chance of beating Crowley.

At that moment Baylin dropped the big bunch of keys which crashed on the hard floor, startling Crowley, and for a split second his attention wavered from Law. He glanced downwards at the keys, but instantly recovered, and was shocked to see that Law had drawn his gun and was set to shoot. His brain sent an emergency signal to his trigger finger, but his reaction was slow. Law's pistol belched flame and smoke and a big .45 slug struck Crowley's right hand.

Crowley dropped the gun as the crash of the shot racketed through the cell block. Blood spurted from his shattered hand. He covered the wound with his left hand and staggered away from the cell door to flop down on the bunk, gazing in horror at his hand and groaning as pain began to flare.

Baylin bent and picked up the bunch of keys. His face was pale but he grinned at Law.

'You didn't think I was gonna unlock

the door, did you?' he asked.

Law grinned. 'You can unlock it now,' he said. 'Crowley needs the attention of the doctor, and I want that gun out of there.'

Baylin unlocked the door and Law entered the cell. He picked up the discarded pistol and found it useless, his bullet having smashed the cylinder as well as Crowley's hand. He checked Crowley's wound, but the ex-deputy had lost all interest in the current situation.

'I'll get the doc to come and look at you,' Law promised, leaving the cell. He paused while Baylin relocked the door, and then they walked back into the office. Someone was knocking at the street door and Baylin hurried to it.

'Who's there?' he called.

'Johnny Shane from the restaurant. I got six breakfasts here for your prisoners.'

'Hold it for a moment.' Baylin moved to the big front window and peered out. He threw a glance at Law and grinned.

'It is Johnny Shane. He brings meals for the prisoners every day.'

Law stood behind the desk as Baylin unlocked the office door and watched a young man carrying two metal containers enter the office, and then, as Baylin began closing the door behind the newcomer, two men holding drawn pistols lunged across the threshold from either side of the doorway. The foremost struck Baylin on the head with his pistol while the other faced Law, who snatched his pistol from its holster. Baylin fell to the floor as Law triggered his Colt, and a blast of fire shook the office.

First one then the other hard case was hit, and neither had the speed to use his gun. They fell in a death-flurry of limbs, and Law stood with ready gun as he watched. He recognized them as two of the three men who had ridden into town as he was checking the dead man in the loft of the livery stable.

'I'm sorry,' said Johnny Shane when the reports of the shooting faded. His face was pale and he was trembling. 'They got the drop on me outside and there was nothing I could do.'

Law went to Baylin's side. The jailer was sitting on the floor holding a hand to his forehead with blood showing through his fingers. Law helped him to his feet, sat him down on a chair, and then told Johnny Shane to fetch the doctor. The youngster ran from the office, and Law satisfied himself that the two men he had shot were dead before going out to the sidewalk to take a look around the street.

He was worried about Julie and Ben Rutherford, but there was no way he could leave town at the moment. He stood looking around, and presently saw Doc Rouse coming towards him, accompanied by Johnny Shane. He reloaded his pistol, eased it into his holster, and went back into the office.

'You've started early this morning,' Doc Rouse commented when he arrived. He went to Baylin's side, examined the jailer, and then said, 'He'll live.'

He turned to the two men on the floor, shaking his head.

'They're beyond your help, Doc,' Law said. 'Crowley needs your attention. He's in a cell with a busted hand.' He glanced at Johnny Shane, who was standing just inside the doorway. 'Close and bolt the door, Johnny. We don't want to be disturbed again.'

He watched the youngster obey, then picked up the cell keys and led the doctor into the cell block. Rouse tut-tutted when he examined Crowley's hand, and set to work instantly on the ex-deputy's wound.

'I'll lock you in while we're feeding the prisoners,' Law said, and did so before calling to Johnny Shane to bring in the food.

Law stood by while the prisoners were fed, opening one cell at a time until the chore was completed. He could hear someone banging on the street door, and went in answer. Peering through the big window, he saw Charlie Cooper of Double C standing on the sidewalk, accompanied by his foreman, Pete Hubbard. Law opened the door with his left hand, his right hand down at his side close to the butt of his holstered pistol.

He could tell by Cooper's face that the rancher had heard the news of his son's death, and was ready for trouble as Cooper came into the office.

'What happened to Leroy?' Cooper demanded.

Law explained tersely and Cooper heaved a long sigh and shook his head.

'He got mixed up with the wrong company,' Cooper said sadly. 'Can I talk to Chance Geest? I'd like to know what really went on with my son, and Chance is the only one who can tell us.'

'Not at the moment.' Law shook his head. 'I haven't got at the truth myself yet. I'm on my own here and I need to be out on the trail. Come back in a couple of days when things have settled down.'

'Where's Leroy's body? Is it at the undertaker's?' Cooper's voice was filled with despair, and his eyes were listless when he met Law's gaze.

'Yes. If you're going along there perhaps you'll tell the undertaker to come and collect two more bodies.'

Cooper turned away and Pete Hubbard followed his boss along the street. Law watched them until they were out of sight. Johnny Shane came to the door, ready to leave.

'Look up the town mayor and tell him I need some dependable men in here to relieve me,' Law instructed. 'Will you do that?'

'Sure, Marshal. Right away.' Shane departed with a clattering of his metal food containers, and set off at a run along the sidewalk.

Law closed the office door and went to Baylin's side. The jailer was slumped in his seat, his eyes closed. Blood was staining the bandage the doctor had applied to his head.

'How you feeling Bill?' Law asked.

'Not good,' Baylin mumbled.

'You'd better go home and rest up,' Law suggested, and Baylin lurched to his feet and departed.

Doc Rouse called from Crowley's cell and Law hurried in answer. Rouse was ready to leave. Crowley was slumped on his bunk, his right hand swathed in a bandage.

'I've done all I can for him,' Rouse said. 'I'll give him another look later.'

Law released the doctor from the cell and followed him into the office. At that moment someone hammered on the street door, and Law went in answer, his gun in his right hand. He opened the door to find a short, fat man confronting him.

'I'm Mike Blair, the mortician,' the newcomer said. 'You're having a busy time of it, Marshal.'

'It happens that way sometimes,' Law replied. 'Come in. I got a couple more for you.'

Blair merely looked in at the two bodies and then nodded. 'I'll get the handcart and my assistant,' he said, and hurried off.

Doc Rouse departed without a word and Law stood in the doorway, inwardly chafing because he could not pursue his own job. He saw the town mayor along the street, accompanied by two men who were joined by a third man as they came towards the law office.

'You need some help,' said the mayor when they arrived. 'These men usually help out the law when extra guns are needed. They'll stand by here until they're relieved. I'll send a report to Sheriff Derry and get some more official help here. OK?'

'Yeah. Thanks.' Law nodded. 'I've got a particular chore to take care of that I can't do while I'm here. I have to ride out.' He looked at the three men with the mayor. 'Just stick around the office, and don't take any chances with the prisoners. I'll be gone most of the morning, I reckon.'

The men entered the office. Law heaved a sigh of relief and departed immediately, heading for the livery barn, but as he passed the restaurant the smell of cooking breakfast caught his nostrils and he turned aside instinctively, aware that he was ravenous. He ordered a meal and forced down his impatience until he had eaten it and swallowed two cups of coffee.

Feeling better for the meal, he went on to the stable and prepared his horse for travel. When he rode out, heading for Circle R, he was aware that he had to check out the ranch in his search for Julie Rutherford before he could even consider any other action. The girl had given him problems from the start but he could not ignore her.

When he reined up on a skyline to look at Circle R he was disappointed to see the spread was seemingly deserted — no horses in the corral and no movement around the buildings. Law remained motionless, thinking about the situation. Ben Rutherford had been kidnapped by two men and taken out of town. Then Julie rode out and had vanished.

He eased back into cover and checked the trail leading into the ranch. There were no recent tracks in the dust, but that didn't prove anything. He moved forward again to study the ranch once more and, while he was motionless, a glint of movement caught his eye from one of the front windows in the house. He produced his field glasses and studied the building, quickly spotting the figure of a man inside, holding a rifle and apparently on guard.

Law eased away until he was out of sight of the house and then began to circle. He rode wide until he reached the rear of the building. He left his horse in thick brush, took his rifle and moved in on foot until he could see the rear of the ranch house.

A horse whinnied nearby, and Law froze in his tracks and looked around intently. He held his rifle in his left hand and placed his right hand on the butt of his holstered pistol. His keen gaze flitted over the rear of the house and the surrounding area, and he soon spotted a buggy roughly concealed in the brush and knew that Julie Rutherford had come home in her search of her father.

Dropping into cover, Law moved to investigate, and when he reached the side of the buggy he found a picket line deeper in the brush with ten horses tied to it. A twig snapped just behind him as he gazed at the horses and he whirled quickly, his right hand lifting his pistol clear of its holster.

He found himself face to face with a small man holding a levelled rifle.

'Don't shoot,' Law rapped. 'I'm looking for Butch Rainey. Scar Crowley told me I'd find him here. Is he around?'

The man peered at him, eyes narrowed, suspicion staining his weathered features.

'He's in the house with the rest of the gang. Who are you?'

'I told you Scar Crowley sent me.

Him and Sam Hoyt are in jail in Buffalo Creek and want to be sprung pronto. The law has cleaned up in town. Strutt and most of Rainey's men there are either dead or in jail.'

'Rainey knows about that and says there ain't nothing he can do.' The guard motioned with his rifle. 'You better go into the house and report to Rainey. The gang is about to pull out. We've been run ragged by a bunch of Texas Rangers, and they're still on our tails, I reckon. We shouldn't have stopped off here but Rainey had a couple of scores to settle.'

'Is Julie Rutherford and her father in the house?' Law queried.

'A gal turned up earlier, driving this buggy,' the guard replied. 'She's been in the house ever since. Rainey's got the rancher inside, trying to make him sign over his ranch with papers Strutt prepared for him.'

Law nodded and half turned away, then swung back to face the man, who was turning to return to the horses.

Law struck with his rifle barrel, slamming it against the man's hat. There was a smothered cry and the man dropped inertly into the tall grass. Law disarmed him quickly and then scouted the immediate area, looking for other guards, and discovered that he was alone with the horses.

He went along the line releasing the animals, waving his hat, slapping rumps until they spooked and ran away from the ranch. They crossed a ridge a hundred yards from the house, running as if they wouldn't stop until they reached the border.

Law returned his attention to the house. He studied the outside of the building, aware that he could not go close because the odds of ten to one were too great and he had no wish to commit suicide. He wondered about Julie and her father. If the couple were still alive in the house their presence would greatly complicate the situation.

The back door opened at that moment and a figure emerged to come running almost directly to where Law was crouched near the buggy. He recognized Julie Rutherford, and she was evidently making for the buggy. Law grinned, and then sobered quickly. A man appeared in the doorway and raised a rifle to draw a bead on the girl's fleeing figure.

Law lifted his rifle into the aim and centred on the man. He fired, clenching his teeth as the shot crashed, throwing harsh echoes to the horizon. The man twisted and fell heavily. Julie halted and looked around like a hunted animal.

'Over here, Julie!' Law yelled, standing up to reveal his presence.

He saw the relief which came to the girl's face as she recognized him, and she came running towards him. Law watched the house behind her. A man stepped into the back doorway and Law fired two shots that dropped him instantly. A side window in the house suddenly shattered and glass tinkled. A rifle barrel appeared, and Law bracketed the window with three shots.

The next instant Julie was in cover beside him. She hurled herself flat behind the buggy and lay gasping for breath. Law watched the house but now it was ominously silent. When Julie had regained her breath she stirred and looked up at him.

'It's Rainey and his rustlers!' she gasped. 'They grabbed me when I got here, and made me cook food for them. They're pulling out shortly because the Rangers are after them, and Rainey said he would kill my father before he left.'

'I know.' Law nodded. 'How'd you get free?'

'I was left alone in the kitchen and ran for it.'

'You better get out of here,' Law said. 'If the Rangers are close by then I'll try and hold Rainey and his men until they arrive.'

'The odds are too great!' Julie gasped. 'There are at least ten rustlers.'

At that moment two men rushed out of the back door and came running towards the buggy. Law raised his rifle, but his attention was distracted by a group of five men that appeared around the front corner of the house and came at a run across open ground.

'They want their horses,' Law said, 'and they don't know yet that I ran them off.'

He started shooting with his rifle, and, as the hammering reports rang out, some of the running men fell to the ground. He concentrated on the five figures to his right, and then shifted his aim to the two on the left. Julie saw the guard's discarded rifle and snatched it up. She dived under the buggy, took cover behind a wheel, and started shooting at the rustlers.

The rustlers fell quickly. Law sent a stream of .44-40 slugs into them and the survivors changed their minds about a frontal assault and went to ground. Law kept watch, shooting at targets as they appeared, while Julie worked the mechanism of the rifle she was holding, determined to kill rustlers.

Shots were fired from the house and Law returned fire, aware that now there were only three men inside, and one of them was the rustler boss himself, Butch Rainey. But Rainey was afoot, cut off from his horse, and that gave Law the advantage. He judged that four of the seven rustlers who had charged from the house were finished, and the remaining three seemed to have lost all interest in fighting.

'Stay here and be ready to run if I lose out,' Law said tensely. 'I'm going over to confront Rainey. I want to get to your father before they think about killing him.'

Law moved out swiftly, running across the open ground, pistol in his right hand now, and he watched for signs of the rustlers as he made for the kitchen door of the ranch house. Two rustlers who had survived the charge from the house began to fire at him and Julie threw lead rapidly in their direction, sending them into cover. Law reached the rear of the house and lunged for the kitchen doorway.

A rustler appeared in the doorway, his gun flaming, and Law ducked at a near miss but did not hesitate. He fired without seeming to aim, and the rustler pitched forward on to his face. Law entered the house and ran towards the front room, gun uplifted. The house shook to the blast of shooting.

Law burst into the big front room overlooking the porch. He saw at a glance that Ben Rutherford was tied to a chair in a corner, apparently unharmed. Two men were at the front windows, their backs to the interior of the room, shooting rapidly out at the yard. Law recognized the big figure of Butch Rainey from the several times he had attempted to end the rustler's crooked career in the past, and shouted to make himself heard above the noise of the shooting, calling for the man's attention.

Rainey swung around, pistol swinging, and Law triggered two quick shots that struck the big rustler dead centre in the chest. Rainey dropped his gun and then followed it to the floor, blood spurting. The second man looked round and then threw down his gun and raised his hands.

The racket of the shots faded slowly. Law moved to a window and peered out, wondering at the shooting in the yard, and saw riders milling about outside. He recognized several of them as Texas Rangers, and holstered his pistol and went to the front door.

Julie came running into the house and threw herself at her father. Law stepped on to the porch and a dozen Ranger guns swung to cover him. He called a greeting to Captain McCall, and heaved a long sigh as full silence returned to the ranch, aware that he had finally shot his way through the crooked business. In the background he could hear Julie talking to her father, and Ben Rutherford was assuring his daughter that he was all right.

Law sat down on the porch step,

feeling suddenly very weary. There were still a number of questions he wanted to get answers to, but in the main he was satisfied with how it had all turned out.

THE END